Rough Around the Edges

The Protectors

Patricia Keelyn

Panther Press

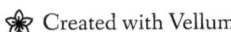 Created with Vellum

For my parents, Peter and Eileen Van Wie, for raising me to believe I could do anything. Even write books.

Special thanks to Ronnie and Barry White, for their insights on Cuban restaurants. To Sharyn Kloster and Dr. Edward White for the medical information. And to Marta Romaguera for checking my Spanish.

As always, Ann, Gin, and Sandra, you made it so much more fun.

Table of Contents

Connections

Welcome to The Protectors Series.

This is a "themed" series where each book stands alone but with a common element. All the heroes are ex-military, who see themselves as protectors for the people in their lives. All five books are romantic suspense, but some are more intense, edgier, with more focus on the suspense than others.

There are, however, two other connections in these books. Two of them, Loving Lindsey and Becca and the Beast, take place in the same small town, Willowbend Wyoming, and they have common characters. Also, the hero in Nobody's Hero appears in one of my Mother's Heart Books, Keeping Katie. I guess there are just some characters and places I can't let go of.

Enjoy, Pat Lewin

Prologue

Alejandro Jamison had never lacked courage. Until now.

Tunneling his fingers into his hair, Alex rested his forehead against the palm of his hand, staring at the large manila envelope lying unopened on his desk.

Two years earlier he'd taken early retirement from the army and put everything he had into a rundown strip of stores in his old neighborhood—the neighborhood where his father had deserted his family, and where an eighteen-year-old Alex had been arrested for breaking and entering. The neighborhood the military had helped him escape.

Buying the buildings had been the beginning of what Alex planned to turn into a safe haven for kids, a community center where no matter how bad their home life, they'd be given a fighting chance. He wanted to do for the young people of this neighborhood what the army had done for him: show them there were ways out. Safe, legal ways.

Now, everything he'd worked for hinged on the contents of an envelope he couldn't bring himself to open.

Pushing back from the desk, he stood and turned toward

the open windows. The damp heat pressed in on him, but he hardly noticed. The heat was familiar, an element he knew and understood. While this other, a system determined to break him now that he was finally playing by its rules, remained incomprehensible.

Absently, he watched several neighborhood kids shooting hoops. The basketball court had been last winter's addition to the center. Several local businesses had donated the materials, and he and a group of older boys had done the work. Afterward, they'd hosted a neighborhood barbecue to celebrate.

Such a small thing: a basketball court.

Yet it had already drastically changed one boy's life. A kid who a year before was restless, bored, and toying with drugs. Now the natural athlete was being scouted by college recruiters and coaching grade-schoolers in the afternoon.

Alex turned back to his desk and picked up the envelope. He couldn't put it off any longer. The fate of the center rested on its contents. Before he could change his mind, he tore it open and read it quickly. Then the form letter crumbled in his fist as his last hope of saving the center faded away.

"Alex, you got to see this."

Startled, he looked up.

LJ Jones, his friend and partner, stood in the office doorway. "Hey, man, you okay?"

Alex pulled himself together. "Fine. What's up?"

LJ, evidently not convinced, hesitated, but finally let it slide. "Come on out and take a look."

Alex followed LJ through the center's main room to the door leading out into the shop area. Several boys hovered around an old Ford Mustang they'd been working on for months. LJ had found it in a junkyard, minus the engine.

Since then, it had been his pet project to teach the boys about repairing engines by guiding them through the building of one.

Now, proud as any new father, he crossed his arms and nodded to one of the boys. "Okay, show the man."

The boy climbed into the old car and turned the key. The engine roared to life, and a cheer of triumph rose from the group standing nearby.

Alex knew then what he had to do.

Fifteen minutes later he picked up the phone and dialed a number from a card he'd nearly tossed away a dozen times. When the man on the other end answered, Alex said, "Sal? Jamison here. I've changed my mind."

"Alex! I knew you'd come around. I said to—"

Alex cut him off. "Just tell me the terms."

"Sure, sure. No problem. A thousand up front. Win or lose. Five if you win."

"Two up front. Seventy-five hundred if I win."

Two thousand wouldn't cut it, but then, he had no intention of losing.

"Can't do it." Alex could almost see the man squirming on the other end of the line. "Not the first time out. You're an unknown."

"Then I take my *talent* elsewhere."

"Hey, Alex, I discovered you. Give me some time. I can make you rich."

"I don't want rich, Sal. I want two thousand up front and seventy-five hundred if I win. Otherwise, there's no deal."

Sal hesitated but evidently thought better of pushing his luck. "Okay, okay, you got it. I'll set it up."

"When?"

"Tomorrow night. I'll pick you up at nine."

"No. You're not to come here. Ever. I'll meet you some-where outside of Miami."

They made arrangements to meet in Ft. Lauderdale, and when Alex hung up the phone, he had to suppress the urge to immediately go wash his hands. He reminded himself why he was doing this: the center and the kids who'd come to depend on it. These kids defined courage, and he couldn't—wouldn't—fail them now. He'd been fighting for months to save this place but had been going about it the wrong way. He'd been playing by the rules.

Now he planned on doing things his way.

Chapter One

Exhaustion had become a way of life.

Through the grueling years of medical school, Dr. Kristen Helton had come to accept that fact. Practicing medicine came with a steep price: long, seemingly never-ending hours. Now, after her first full day at the Miami Hope Medical Clinic, she realized things weren't going to change. She loved her work, but it demanded every ounce of her energy.

Fatigue pulling at her, she stepped outside and took a deep breath. When she'd walked through the clinic's doors fourteen hours earlier, the sun had not yet risen above the gray waters of the Atlantic. Now light leaked from the sky, streaking the western horizon with splashes of rose and lavender.

Kristen stood transfixed, struck by the beauty of the sunset and the only daylight she'd experienced in the past twenty-four hours. The city, too, seemed to hold its breath, the heat hanging heavily in the air, waiting for the day to sink into the relative coolness of night.

Without further hesitation, Kristen started down the

street. It wasn't a long walk to the vacant corner lot where the clinic's patients and personnel parked, but she preferred making it in the daylight. It was safer. Of course, safety was a relative state. Most of her colleagues considered her crazy for practicing in this section of Miami—no matter the time of day.

The neighborhood had once been a thriving working-class community of old-style Florida homes in shades of pastel pink and peach. But time and neglect had wreaked their havoc. Everyone who could afford it had long since moved north into Broward and Palm Beach counties, leaving the neighborhood to those who couldn't escape. Now the houses were dingy with age, paint peeling and walls rust-stained from years of watering once-sodded lawns that now consisted mostly of sand spurs, weeds, and the roots of massive, overgrown ficus trees.

The clinic sat near the center of a long block, just another flat-roofed house with wrought-iron bars on its jalousie windows, remodeled to serve as a free outpatient medical center for the neighborhood. As she came abreast of the house two doors down, she noticed four teenage boys hanging out in the front yard. One sat on the edge of a beat-up old car while the others hovered around him like pups near a hound.

A flicker of uneasiness stirred her stomach, but Kristen pushed it aside. After all, if she was going to continue practicing medicine at the Hope Clinic, she couldn't let fear of the people who lived in this neighborhood deter her. Forcing a smile, she nodded and kept walking.

A wolf whistle split the air.

Embarrassment heated her cheeks, and renewed wariness shot through her. She was twice those boys' age and knew they were just making fun, trying to get a reaction out of her. Still . . .

"Hey, pretty lady," called a male voice from the yard. "Where you headed?"

Ignore them, she told herself. Advice that would have been easier to take if she hadn't sensed movement behind her. They were following her. Without looking back, she tightened her hold on her purse strap and picked up her pace.

"Hey, *chica,* what's your hurry?"

She told herself she wasn't afraid. But it took effort not to run. Even though she knew that would be a mistake, letting them see that they'd gotten to her. Frightened her. Besides, she was almost at the vacant lot where she'd left her car. She passed the last house, started across the sandy driveway, and stopped.

Her car was gone.

For a moment, she could only stand and stare, unwilling to believe what her eyes were telling her. Someone had stolen her car.

"You lose something, *chica?"*

The taunting voice snapped her out of her inertia, and she spun around. All four boys had followed her, but the one who'd been sitting on the car was close enough to touch. Before she could stop herself, she took a step back.

He was probably only sixteen or seventeen and wasn't very tall—maybe five six or seven. But Kristen doubted he needed either height or age to exert his authority. His shoulders and arms would have been formidable on a grown man, and his eyes . . . his eyes looked decades older than the rest of him.

It took all her willpower to keep from backing farther away. "Why are you following me?" she asked.

He grinned, but there was no amusement in his dark eyes. "Why, we're just trying to be good citizens."

"Yeah," jeered one of the other boys. "We're doin' our civic duty."

Kristen glanced from one to the other. "I appreciate your concern, but I'm fine, thank you."

"Looks to me like you're lost." The leader stuffed his hands into a pair of worn, skin-tight jeans, and the others spread out, circling her. "What you think, *amigos*? The *chica* look lost to you?"

"I'm not lost." She glanced around, hoping to spot someone else—some adult—who might come to her aid. There was no one. She was on her own. "I'm a doctor at the clinic down the street," she said, keeping her voice firm and steady. "Now, if you'll excuse me." She started to move past him while slipping her hand inside her purse to grab her cell phone.

He stepped in her path.

For the first time, real fear gripped her even as her fingers brushed the cool metal of her phone. If this was supposed to be fun and games, she wasn't laughing. While struggling to keep from panicking, she used her most authoritative voice and pulled the cell from her bag. "Get out of my way."

The boy reached out and grabbed her arm. "Now, why would I want to do that?"

* * *

Alex grinned as he spotted Carlos, one of the older boys, on the basketball court practicing his shots. It had been the worst kind of day, filled with paperwork and bureaucrats. Yanking at his tie, Alex headed toward the court. A few rounds of one on one might be just the thing to clear his head and work the kinks from his joints.

"Okay, Carlos . . ." Alex tossed his shirt and tie across a nearby fence and dodged in to grab the ball from the teenager. "Let's see just how good you are."

Carlos rolled his eyes and jogged after him. "Hey, man, you want to get your ass beat, ain't no skin off my hide."

He was probably right, Alex thought. The kid was a natural on the court, while Alex's physical skills took a different, less wholesome bent. But, hey, he'd take the lanky teenager showing him up any day over the polite hand-shakes and insincere smiles he'd endured these past few hours.

"We'll see about that," Alex said as he made it to the end of the court and sank the ball. "One nothing."

Carlos snagged the ball as it fell through the net and started back down the court. "Enjoy your point. It's the only one you're gonna get."

Alex laughed and followed the boy as he dribbled to the opposite end of the court and easily made the shot. Alex reclaimed the ball and lost it again before finally getting his hands on it and heading back toward the net.

"Alex!"

Stopping mid-dribble, he swiveled toward the young boy running toward him. "What is it, Miguel?"

"There's trouble over on the lot."

Alex tossed the ball to Carlos and started toward the younger boy. "What kind of trouble?"

"Hector's got some woman cornered."

"A woman?"

"A stranger."

"Damn." More trouble was the last thing the neighbor-hood needed. It brought focus to the area in the form of police and bad publicity. Then they'd have a rash of do-gooders descending on them applying Band-Aids to problems they couldn't begin to understand.

Alex grabbed his shirt and pulled it on. "Miguel, stay here with Carlos." It was one thing for Alex to get into it with Hector, and quite another for one of the boys.

"We aren't going anywhere," Carlos said, dropping a hand on Miguel's shoulder. "I don't have any argument with Hector and mean to keep it that way."

Alex nodded, knowing Carlos would keep a tight leash on the younger boy, and took off toward the front of the building.

From half a block away Alex could tell the woman didn't belong on his streets. Her expensive clothes would have made her conspicuous even if her pale skin and deep red hair had not.

A perfect target for Hector and his gang.

Still, Alex hesitated to interfere until it was absolutely necessary. Hector was a born leader who already held sway over too many of the neighborhood's youth. The wrong move from Alex could send the kids sitting on the fence scurrying in Hector's direction. Besides, Alex wanted to give the boy a chance to back away from the woman on his own.

Then Hector grabbed her arm.

Kristen dropped her phone and heard it hit the pavement.

"Let go of me." She looked away from the hand gripping her wrist into the boy's face. The sharp intelligence in his eyes didn't surprise her, but the emotion did, stunning her with its intensity. And for a moment she forgot her fear as she wondered what had made him so angry.

Suddenly the boy shifted to look at something behind her.

"What's going on, Hector?"

Relief washed through her at the sound of the deep voice, and she twisted around to see the man who'd come up behind her.

He dwarfed them both, making her instantly aware of the differences between the boy holding on to her wrist and an adult male. The boy called Hector didn't stand a chance. Though he obviously didn't quite see it that way, because he glared defiantly at the older man.

"You go on back to your rocking chair, old man," he said. "You aren't needed here. I got things under control."

Though the man didn't budge, he seemed to loom larger. "I *asked* you a question."

A flicker of uncertainty crossed Hector's face, but it vanished as quickly as it had surfaced. "I'm helping the lady out. You know how it is."

The man lowered his gaze to Hector's hand still holding her wrist. "The lady doesn't seem too thrilled with your help."

"Sometimes *gringos* don't know what's good for them."

The man glanced at her briefly before focusing on the boy. "Let her go, Hector." It was a command, one not meant to be ignored.

The other boys had backed off, but Hector wasn't so easily intimidated. "Why are you always sticking your nose into places you are not wanted?"

The man took a step forward, and Hector opened his hand and backed up. "Okay," he said. "I let her go. You happy?"

Kristen quickly moved out of the way, rubbing her wrist, and then quickly retrieved her phone from the ground. Fortunately, it didn't look damaged.

"Yeah," the man said. "I'm happy."

"Then tell her to get out of here and not come back. We don't need her kind around here." He spit on the ground and nodded toward his friends, and the four of them trotted off in the direction they'd come.

Kristen watched them go, and then turned to her rescuer. "Thank you . . ." she started, but stopped when she caught the disapproval on the man's face. For a moment, she wondered if she'd been better off dealing with Hector and his friends; then dismissed the idea. She couldn't expect this man to be all smiles after his encounter with the four young hoods. "Thank you," she said again. "I'm not sure I could have handled them on my own."

"Hector's right. You don't belong here."

Again, his manner took her aback. "I'm a doctor at the Hope Clinic down the street." She hated that her voice sounded defensive.

"That's a half block away. What are you doing way up here?"

"Not that it's any of your business, but there's no room for cars down at the clinic. This is where I was told to park."

"Then I suggest you take Hector's advice and get in your car and leave."

"I would if I could. But someone stole it."

"Someone stole your car?" It was almost as if he didn't believe her.

"It certainly seems that way," she said, trying and failing to keep her sarcasm in check. "I parked it here this morning, and it's not here now."

He glanced around the lot, shaking his head, before

turning back to her. "Come on," he said, taking her arm and starting toward the sidewalk.

It took Kristen a few steps to get over her shock enough to pull away from him. "Wait a minute. I'm not going anywhere with you." She lifted her cell phone to bring it to his attention. "I'll call from here."

"Look," he said. "Hector isn't the worst this neighborhood has to offer. The next welcoming committee might not be so courteous. You need to get off the streets. Come on."

Kristen glanced in the direction he indicated and saw only a strip mall. "Forget it."

"It's a youth center, and there are at least two dozen people in the building. You'll be safe while you call the police about your car."

Kristen looked again at the building across the street, noticing the bright lights inside and out. At some point during her encounter with the boys, full darkness had fallen. She glanced back toward the clinic and realized she didn't want to walk back past the house where she'd first seen them. It seemed like her best option was to accept this man's questionable hospitality.

Turning back to him, she said, "Okay. Let's go."

As she followed him across the street, she stole a sideways glance at her rescuer.

Like the boy, it wasn't his height that set him apart, but something else. Something less easily defined. A certain intensity in his black eyes, or the grim set of his dark features perhaps. Kristen wasn't sure. Certainly, no one would call him a handsome man, not in the conventional sense anyway. But he was compelling, drawing a woman's eyes with the dark magnetism in his gaze, making her want to brush her fingers across his brow to ease the tension there.

13

Looking away from him, she quickly suppressed that last thought. This man, whoever he was, wasn't the type to let a woman get that close. Besides, she still wasn't sure that she wouldn't have been safer on her own. There were worse forms of danger than the physical.

Chapter Two

Alex avoided touching her again.

Once had been enough. He didn't need another contact with her smooth skin or the delicate bones beneath it. She was the kind of woman who spelled trouble, an outsider with more money than common sense. And Alex knew better than to even look at her.

He already had enough problems.

So, as they crossed the street and made their way toward the center, he kept his distance.

"You haven't told me your name," she said as they approached the entrance to the converted buildings.

He stopped with his hand on the door and looked at her. The center's lights reflected off her pale skin, and, despite his earlier resolve, he saw that her eyes were green: clear emerald green. "Alex," he answered abruptly, irritated with himself for noticing something as pointless as her eye color. "Alex Jamison."

She held out her hand. "Kristen Helton."

He considered ignoring the overture but found himself enclosing her small hand in his instead. "Dr. Helton."

"Call me Kristen, please." She smiled, a soft, tentative smile that stirred his senses and sent warning signals straight to his groin.

She was trouble, definitely trouble.

Releasing her hand, he nodded—though he had no intention of using her first name. He opened the door and motioned for her to precede him inside. She stepped across the threshold and stopped, her gaze wandering over the center's main room.

Alex came in behind her and tried to picture the way she saw the center. The old shopping strip had once contained four stores, but the first thing he'd done was knock down the inside walls to create one large, open area. Then he'd divided the space into modular units using furniture groupings, with each section devoted to something the kids needed or wanted—education or entertainment. He believed in the concept, but everything about the place was rough. Most of the materials had been donated by small local business owners, and most of the work had been done by him or LJ. He had no doubt it was a far cry from Dr. Helton's usual surroundings.

"It's not what I expected," she said.

He couldn't tell whether her comment held censorship or approval, but he'd bet on the former.

"The idea is to avoid any closed areas where a kid can go off on his own and hide," he said, surprising himself that he'd bothered to explain.

"Is that usually a problem?"

Alex shrugged. "It can be. Kids in neighborhoods like this one, where there's little money and even less parental supervision, tend to go one of two ways. Either they join one of the local gangs in order to be part of a group, or they become loners."

"That sounds like typical teenage behavior."

"Maybe. But *here,* either extreme can be dangerous. You've seen what a gang like Hector's can become. And the loners—" He hesitated and slipped his hands into his pockets. "Well, they can cause even more trouble. We're trying to show these kids that being part of something is good, that there's strength in working together. *If* it's the right group."

He realized suddenly that he'd said more than he'd planned. He'd brought her here to use her phone in a safe environment, nothing more. Instead, he'd ended up talking about his outlook on helping kids. And for some reason he couldn't explain, it seemed important that she understand.

"The office is this way," he said without elaborating further. "You can make your call from there." He led her across the room to his office, ignoring the curious stares of a half dozen boys. Pointing through the plate-glass window toward his desk, he said, "I'll wait out here."

She went inside, and he turned away, wondering what had gotten into him. Not that he wasn't known for spouting off to anyone who'd listen about the importance of providing a place like the center for kids in low-income neighborhoods. Hell, he'd just spent the better part of his day doing that for a bunch of money men.

Taking money from the rich was one thing; letting them near his boys was something else again. He knew too well the havoc someone like Dr. Helton could wreak with her guilty conscience and upscale ways. She'd stay for a while, pretending to care, then split when things got rough—usually about the time some poor sucker had come to depend on her.

"Alex!"

Startled from his thoughts, Alex turned to see LJ bearing down on him, looking like a man on a mission.

17

"We need to talk," he said.

Alex had known this was coming. Sooner or later, LJ was bound to notice the extra cash Alex was putting into the center. However, he'd hoped he would have a little more time before having to come up with an explanation. Though he doubted there would *ever* be a good time. "Later, LJ."

Crossing his arms, LJ parked himself squarely in front of Alex. "This can't wait."

"It's going to have to." Alex nodded toward the office and the woman talking on her phone. "Unless you want to have this conversation in front of an audience."

LJ glanced through the window and scowled. "Who is she?"

"Dr. Kristen Helton. She's new down at the clinic."

"Another one? How many does that make this year? Three?"

"Four. You're forgetting the guy who lasted less than a week."

"So"—LJ shook his head—"what's she doing here?"

"Reporting her stolen car to the police."

LJ frowned. "Why call from here? Why not call from the clinic?"

"She probably would have. Except she had a little run-in with Hector Gonzales and his gang."

"Damn! And you got involved. Right?"

"What was I supposed to do?" Alex demanded, a flush of anger sweeping through him. "Stand by and watch Hector manhandle her?"

LJ instantly looked contrite. "Okay, I'm sorry. That came out wrong. I know you did what you had to. What anyone would have done in the same circumstance. It's just—"

"I know . . ." Alex's anger vanished as quickly as it had

surfaced. "Throwing my weight around with Hector isn't a good idea. No doubt it'll come back to haunt me just like the last time. I certainly haven't done anything right with that boy yet."

"You didn't have a choice."

"Not today maybe, but before . . ." Alex shrugged. "I'm not so sure." He understood all too well the anger blinding Hector's judgment, but Alex couldn't get through to the boy no matter how hard he tried. "There has got to be a way to reach him."

"That kid is serious trouble," LJ said. "It's time you faced that."

"Maybe." Alex rested his hands on his hips and let his gaze wander across the room. "I just keep thinking there's more to him than meets the eye."

"There's more all right. More meanness."

This wasn't the first time they'd had this conversation. While Alex maintained that underneath Hector's tough, angry exterior was a good heart, LJ believed the boy was bad through and through. But then, LJ hadn't grown up in a neighborhood where a tough mouth and tougher attitude meant the difference between survival and extinction.

"Alejandro, my friend"—LJ rested a hand on Alex's shoulder—"you can't save them all."

Alex saw the sadness in LJ's eyes and knew on some level he was right. "I can try."

"Am I interrupting something?"

Both men turned. Kristen stood in the office doorway, her refined good looks a sharp contrast to the makeshift office behind her.

Knowing his friend's weakness for a pretty face, Alex threw LJ a warning glance. "Nothing that can't wait," he said. "Dr. Helton, this is my partner, LJ Jones. LJ, Dr. Helton."

"It's good to meet you, LJ." She held out her hand and smiled.

Alex mentally groaned as LJ's rough mannerisms melted away.

"The pleasure is all mine, Dr. Helton," he said, taking her hand. "You'll certainly brighten up this rather dull neighborhood."

"Oh, I don't know. So far . . ." She laughed lightly and glanced at Alex. "It seems anything but dull." Then, turning back to LJ, she added, "And, please, call me Kristen."

"Kristen it is." LJ grinned while still holding onto her hand. "Sorry to hear about your car."

"Thank you, it's—"

Alex cleared his throat. "Dr. Helton, did you talk to the police?"

She turned toward Alex, and LJ finally released her hand. "They said they'd be here as soon as possible."

"Which means anytime in the next twenty-four hours," LJ said, sarcasm in his voice.

Alex shot him another warning look. "Let's hope it doesn't take that long." The sooner she was out of there, the better. "Meanwhile, you can wait in the office."

"I've got a better idea, Kristen," LJ said. "Why don't you let me show you around?"

Alex looked again at his friend and partner, who smiled, as if oblivious of Alex's unspoken warnings. Obviously, LJ wasn't nearly as eager to get rid of Dr. Kristen Helton as he should be. And though Alex didn't like the idea of the other man showing her around, he couldn't very well object without raising a few eyebrows.

"I have some work to do," he said more abruptly than he'd intended. "If you need anything, I'll be inside."

Kristen looked at him for a moment before once again turning that smile on LJ. "Where do we start?"

Grinning from ear to ear, LJ led her away.

Alex retreated to his office, where he intended to open the day's mail, but ended up watching them instead. They walked around the center's main room, stopping in each section, where he imagined his partner elaborating on its purpose.

Alex couldn't lie to himself.

Watching the two of them together bothered him. Though at first he told himself it was LJ who concerned him. LJ, who'd grown up in a middle-class neighborhood with middle-class parents, didn't understand the danger of getting to know a woman like Dr. Helton. All he saw was the pretty face with the clear green eyes. And that smile. Damn, that smile alone could bring a man to his knees.

That's when Alex had to admit the truth.

It wasn't just LJ's welfare that concerned Alex. It was his own. Despite everything, he wanted to be the one showing Dr. Kristen Helton around.

* * *

It was in the middle of LJ's explanation about the remedial classes offered by the youth center that Kristen noticed the stranger, a tall blond man, entering Alex's office. Cutting LJ off mid-sentence, she nodded toward the newcomer.

"Who's he?" she asked.

"Detective Frank Langford."

She heard the distaste in LJ's voice and, curious, started across the room. She stopped just outside the doorway, LJ behind her, watching as the newcomer slipped his hands into his pockets and said, "So where's the woman who lost her car?"

"Stolen, Langford." Alex leaned forward in his chair and frowned. "The doctor's car was stolen."

"Okay, stolen." Detective Langford shrugged. "Where is she?"

Kristen stepped into the office. "I'm right here, Detective."

She glanced from him to Alex, who had once again leaned back in his chair, his posture deceptively casual behind the scarred wooden desk. Tension coiled between the two men

Physically, they were opposites.

Frank Langford was tall, well-built, and possessed the kind of blond, blue-eyed good looks that thrived on the South Florida beaches. No doubt he'd broken a few teenage hearts in his youth. Also, he was well groomed, not expensively, but meticulously. He wore nicely tailored suit pants, an immaculate white shirt, and a pin-striped tie. To her, he looked more like a struggling young lawyer than a police detective.

Motioning toward a chair, he said, "Have a seat, Miss—"

"It's Doctor," she informed him. "Dr. Helton."

"Sure thing." Annoyance brushed his features, and she realized he wasn't a man who liked being corrected. "Dr. Helton."

"Isn't it unusual for a detective to answer this kind of call?" She settled into a chair. "I expected a patrolman."

"I was in the neighborhood."

Kristen arched an eyebrow, not believing him. There was something going on here, something between him and Alex. But how it affected her, or why he was here about her car, remained a mystery. "Okay, then, what do you need to know?"

He pulled out a pad and pen and looked pointedly at Alex before focusing back on her. "Maybe we should do this in private."

Kristen settled back in her chair and met his pale gaze. "I couldn't possibly ask Mr. Jamison or Mr. Jones to vacate their office."

Detective Langford frowned. "Whatever makes you more comfortable."

"Thank you."

It seemed to take forever for him to get all the information he needed. He asked the same questions over and over, questions that seemed to have no bearing on her missing car. Midway through her second description of the vehicle, where she'd parked it, and when, two patrolmen showed up. She supposed she should have been surprised, since Detective Langford had implied he'd been sent to take the call, but she wasn't. She'd already decided something wasn't right here, and it had nothing to do with her car. So she went through an abbreviated version of the story once again for the uniformed officers.

Unfortunately, even after they left, Frank Langford lingered. "One more question," he said, picking up his jacket and folding it over his arm. "How did Jamison get involved?"

Kristen hesitated, glancing at Alex before answering. She'd purposely left out any reference to the boys who'd taunted her. "He was passing by and offered to let me use his office to call the police." It wasn't exactly a lie, just not the whole truth.

"Passing by?"

"The clinic's parking lot is right across the street," Alex

said, speaking up for the first time since Kristen had entered the office. "I'd just gotten back from downtown."

Detective Langford ignored him. "I don't understand why you didn't go back down to the clinic, Dr. Helton."

She glanced again at Alex. "The center was closer."

"Uh-huh."

"Look, Officer . . ." She met and holding his gaze. "What difference does it make where I called you from? My car is missing."

"It's Detective," he corrected her, his eyes hard and cold. "And you shouldn't have driven a car like that into this neighborhood. Let's see"—he referred to his notes—"a light blue Mercedes coupe. Current model year."

Kristen bit back her anger and the first sharp retort that sprang to her lips. "Thank you for the advice," she said instead. "I'll keep it in mind." Standing, she added, "Now, if we're done, I'd like to go home."

"Yeah, I guess we're done for now. You need a ride?"

"I'll see that Dr. Helton gets home," Alex said.

Kristen looked at him, making sure her surprise didn't show on her face. "I'd appreciate that."

"I'll be glad to drop you off," Detective Langford offered.

She kept her eyes on Alex, hoping he wouldn't change his mind.

"Don't trouble yourself," Alex said. "I'm going out anyway. I'll take her home."

Kristen let out a breath of relief, wondering what was wrong with her. Alex Jamison was the type of man parents warned their daughters to stay clear of. He was dark, mysterious, and inherently dangerous. Besides that, he'd made it clear he wasn't exactly thrilled with having to deal with her.

So what had she done? She'd accepted *his* offer of a ride over that of a police officer.

She must be crazy.

* * *

The drive from the youth center to Kristen's ocean-side condominium wasn't long. Not in miles anyway. Economically, it might as well have been on the other side of the world.

Born and raised on the ocean side of Palm Beach, Kristen had always been uncomfortably aware of the privilege her family's name and money afforded her. But never as acutely as she was now. They left the squalid neighborhood of boxlike houses and wove their way through the dark streets of downtown Miami. Then they pulled onto the Julia Tuttle Causeway, which stretched across Biscayne Bay connecting Miami to Miami Beach.

She could only imagine Alex's thoughts as he drove, the lights of Miami Beach strung out in front of them like a million loose pearls scattered against the tropical night sky. Except for the directions she'd given him, neither of them had spoken since leaving the center.

Finally, he broke the silence. "Why didn't you tell Langford about Hector?"

The question surprised her. Although she'd purposely not mentioned her unpleasant encounter with Hector to the police, she hadn't really thought about why.

After a moment she said, "There didn't seem any point. Hector didn't strike me as stupid. No way he would have hung around if he and his friends had stolen my car."

"Langford wouldn't be so sure of that." Alex threw her a

sideways glance. "And even if *you* are, you still could have told him about Hector harassing you."

"Is that what you expected me to do?"

She sensed his internal debate before he said, "Yes."

His admission stung, though she knew it shouldn't have. She was as much an unknown to him as he was to her. Besides, until he'd asked the question, she hadn't known herself why she didn't tell the police about the boys.

"It would only have made matters worse the next time I ran into Hector or one of his friends," she said, but that wasn't the only reason. "I didn't like him." Then, realizing Alex might not know who she meant, she added, "Detective Langford."

He laughed abruptly.

She had to look at him then. In the dark, she couldn't see much—only his profile silhouetted against the darkness of sky and water beyond the car window. Then a ribbon of light from a passing car lit his face, revealing the strong features and the shadow of a smile that still haunted his face.

Something inside her shifted.

She'd thought earlier that he wasn't conventionally handsome, and maybe that was true. But this man was more than handsome, more than physically attractive. He drew you in. On one level he was darkly compelling, but that was only a small part of his appeal. There was an energy and strength to him, an uncompromising intensity that demanded attention.

Alex Jamison would be hated or loved, but never ignored.

Which reminded her of the tension between him and Detective Langford. "What's between you two anyway?" she asked.

He glanced at her, obviously puzzled. "Between us?"

"You and Detective Langford. It's pretty obvious you two aren't exactly bosom buddies."

He shook his head. "It's an old story. And a long one."

"I like stories." She shifted sideways in the seat to face him. "Old or otherwise."

He glanced at her briefly. "Why do you want to know?"

"Just curious. Consider it my reward for not ratting on Hector."

For several moments he didn't respond, and Kristen figured that was the end of it. He wasn't going to tell her anything.

Then he surprised her.

"I've known Frankie since we were kids," he said. "We grew up in the neighborhood, went to the same schools, knew the same kids. That sort of thing."

"I take it you weren't friends then either."

"No, we were *never* friends. Though for years we tolerated each other from a distance." He shrugged. "Then Frankie started to run with a bunch called the LoBoys."

"A gang?"

Again, he glanced at her. "You seem surprised."

"He's a police officer."

"Yeah, well, Frankie always was full of surprises. And he always had a thing about control."

"What about you? Were you in this gang?"

"That was part of the problem. I didn't have any use for the LoBoys, or any other gang for that matter."

Somehow that didn't surprise her. He didn't seem like the kind of man who ran with the crowd—even if he was leading it.

"So what happened?"

He shrugged. "We both grew up and took our own paths."

"No, I mean where does all the animosity come from?"

"I told you, Frankie didn't take too well to my refusing to join the LoBoys."

"Surely there's more to it than that."

"Some differences don't go away because of time."

She knew he was leaving something out. The hostility she'd sensed between the two men went far beyond simple adolescent rivalry. Something more had happened between them. She thought about pushing him for more answers but decided against it. After all, she barely knew this man. How could she expect him to confide in her?

Once again, the silence settled around them as they left the causeway behind and turned north on Collins Avenue. They passed the Fontainebleau and Eden Roc, then pulled up under the portico of her ocean-side building.

The doorman started toward them, but she waved him away. Turning to face Alex, she said, "Thank you again for everything. I hope—"

He cut her off. "Langford was right, you know. You never should have parked your car in that lot."

She sighed, tired of all the advice she'd received that day. Well-meaning and otherwise. "Yes, I know."

"And Hector was right too. You don't belong in that neighborhood."

"Really?" she snapped. "I suppose you think I belong here." She nodded toward the building looming beside them.

"Don't you?"

"Thank you for the ride." She reached for the door handle, but he stopped her with a hand on her arm.

"You're a nice lady, Dr. Helton. But you should find somewhere else to practice medicine."

Kristen climbed out of the car and slammed the door before she could say something she might regret later. Something like "Go to hell."

* * *

The center was dark when Alex got back.

He let himself in the side door and locked it behind him. He noticed a couple of boys asleep on couches as he worked his way through the main room to his office. Inside, he turned on the desk lamp and settled into his chair.

"About time you got back."

Alex nearly jumped out of his skin. He swung around to face LJ sitting on the couch. "Man, you just shortened my life by about ten years."

"You get the lady doctor home safe and sound?"

Alex took a deep breath and settled back into his chair. "Yeah."

"Think she'll be back?"

"Don't know." It was a question he'd been asking himself since dropping her off. And if he were honest, he'd admit he wasn't sure what he wanted the answer to be. "Not if she's smart."

An awkward silence fell between them, and then LJ said, "I've been waiting to have that chat I mentioned earlier."

"So, talk." Alex knew damn well where this conversation was going and didn't like it. Unfortunately, he didn't know how to avoid it.

"There were a couple of workmen here today. They said you hired them to install the sprinkler system."

"That's right." It was one of the code violations that would end up shutting down the center if it wasn't fixed. "Did they finish?"

"Yeah, they finished."

"Good." Alex leaned back in his chair, keeping his eyes on the other man. "Looks like we're still in business."

"Where did you get the money?" Leave it to LJ to come straight to the point.

"Does it matter?"

"Hell yes, it matters." LJ came out of his chair in one swift movement. "What are you involved in, Alex?"

"Leave it be, LJ."

LJ rested his hands on the desk and leaned toward him. "Tell me you're not into something illegal. Something that vulture Langford can hang you for."

Alex stood and stared at his friend. "It doesn't concern you." Then he turned and walked out, leaving LJ behind and hating himself every step of the way.

Chapter Three

After letting herself into her condo, Kristen made her way across the dimly lit apartment to the French doors opening onto the penthouse terrace. Outside, she skirted the gardens and pool area and headed toward the chest-high concrete wall that edged the balcony. She couldn't see much of the ocean, only the unbroken darkness of water and sky meeting at some distant point that was the horizon. The shoreline, however, was alive, brightly lit, and extending in both directions on either side of her.

She remembered when she'd first realized she wanted to become a doctor. She couldn't have been more than seven or eight. She'd gone with her mother to a woman's clinic, where her mother, a former nurse, sometimes helped out. Kristen had always liked going places with her mother, but up until then, trips to the clinic had meant no more to Kristen than any other excursion.

That day, she'd felt the difference the moment they stepped through the clinic's doors. The waiting area, usually boisterous and overflowing with women and small children, was unnaturally still. Although a dozen or more people occupied the room, everyone, even the smallest child, watched silently, breathlessly, as one of the doctors crouched on the floor next to a toddler.

Kristen's mother moved quickly to the man's side, leaving Kristen to stare first at the small blue face, and then at the little girl's mother as she watched her small daughter struggle for breath.

Suddenly the doctor pulled something from the child's throat. Air rushed into her lungs, she coughed, and immediately started crying as her mother pulled her into her arms.

Pandemonium broke out as everyone laughed and cried and cheered the doctor. The girl's mother, tears of relief replacing the fear that had been there moments earlier, rocked and crooned to the frightened child.

Now, with years of schooling behind her, Kristen understood the medical details of what had happened that day. If the doctor hadn't been able to extract the toy from the girl's throat, he would have performed an emergency tracheotomy. As a doctor, Kristen realized that under the circumstances, being in a medical clinic surrounded by trained medical personnel, the child's life had never been really in question.

But knowing all that made no difference. Because even now, Kristen's reaction to the incident was the same as it had been that day. Purely emotional. Pure joy at watching someone save a child and bring tears of happiness to a mother's face. Just as she had over twenty years ago, Kristen couldn't think of a better way to spend her life.

She took a deep breath, inhaling the warm ocean scent. Even at midnight, the air that touched her cheeks held remnants of the day's heat. She'd always loved the South Florida weather: the oppressive August humidity and the delicate coolness of January. She'd missed both while away at school in Boston and was grateful to be back . . . and finally practicing medicine.

Today, working at the clinic, had been better than she'd hoped. It had brought her dreams to life. She'd wanted the madness and satisfaction of caring for people who truly needed her, rather than the safety of a cushy practice. And that's what she'd gotten.

If only it were that simple.

She thought about the boys who'd cornered her in the parking lot. She could admit it now—she'd never been more frightened than when Hector had grabbed her arm. She wanted to believe he wouldn't have carried his little game too far. But she couldn't be sure.

Thank God for Alex.

Though thinking about him wasn't much of a comfort. In fact, it disturbed her more than wondering what might have happened if he hadn't shown up.

Turning away from the view, she settled onto a lounge chair, her thoughts scattering in a half-dozen directions. Eventually, they came back to the man. To Alex Jamison.

There was danger in thinking about him. But there was nothing to be done about it. He crowded her thoughts, turning her determination to work at the Hope Clinic into a different type of desire. Something more elemental. Something frightening in its power and the quickness with which it had taken hold of her.

He was an enigma who tempted her to look further, delve deeper. But she couldn't let him get in her way. Just like she couldn't let her fear of all the Hectors out there frighten her. She'd been working toward practicing medicine at a place like the Hope Clinic since that day she'd watched a doctor save a small child's life. She couldn't allow anything, not the danger or her unreasonable preoccupation with the mysterious Alex Jamison, stop her.

* * *

It was late afternoon of the next day before Kristen got back to the youth center. She parked her rental car in front, and, hearing voices, circled around to the back of the building.

Alex and three boys were deeply immersed in a basketball game. She didn't know much about the game, but they seemed to have paired off two against two. But it wasn't the game or the boys that drew her attention. It was Alex.

Watching him was enough to take any woman's breath away, and Kristen wasn't immune. At first she thought he had the body of a well-trained athlete, but that wasn't quite right. He wore cutoffs and a sleeveless blue T-shirt that revealed the tanned, corded muscles of his arms and legs. Maybe the strength she saw in him came from physical labor, but she didn't think so. Not entirely anyway. His movements were too controlled, too precise. In some ways, he seemed out of place on a basketball court with three teenagers. There was something about him, something larger than life, a power that was evident in every step, every pivot and jump, every shift and block. Yet he smiled and laughed, and she sensed that being with these boys came as naturally as breathing to him.

She realized it was the first time she'd seen him really smile, and it made her wonder what it would take to get him to look at her that way. She quickly suppressed the thought. That morning, she'd decided she needed his help to gain acceptance in this neighborhood. Nothing more.

He didn't acknowledge her until they'd finished their game, though she knew he'd spotted her when she'd arrived.

Maybe he thought if he ignored her she would go away. But Kristen had already decided she wasn't going anywhere. Some things were worth fighting for, and she was beginning to think if she wanted to continue at the Hope Clinic, Alex Jamison's acceptance might be one of them.

Finally, the game ended with shouts of triumph and high-fives, and he couldn't ignore her any longer. Grabbing a towel off a nearby fence, he wiped his face as he walked toward her and stopped, draping the cloth around his neck, his expression unreadable.

"Good game," she said, uncomfortably aware of his powerful arms and legs, and the way his damp T-shirt clung to the hard ridges of his chest.

"I thought you'd learned your lesson."

"What lesson is that?" She smiled and feigned ignorance, knowing full well what he referred to.

"That you don't belong here."

"Maybe. But I *am* needed."

He grunted in disgust, and shaking his head, stepped past her, heading for the door.

She turned to follow him. "I'm not easily frightened."

"Too bad." He opened the door, and this time didn't wait for her to go first.

She caught the door and trailed him inside. "Why's that?"

He glanced back at her, seeming surprised that she was still behind him. "Because this neighborhood can be very dangerous. Especially for someone like you."

"Someone like me?"

He stopped suddenly and turned, his dark eyes looking her up and down. "An outsider."

She stiffened and met his gaze. "I can take care of myself."

"Like you did yesterday with Hector?"

Heat flooded her cheeks. "That was a mistake. I won't make the same one again."

"Maybe not, but you'll make others. And I might not be around next time to save your butt." He turned and started walking again.

She followed him into the office. "That's not your problem."

"You got it, babe. It ain't my problem." Grabbing the ends of his shirt, he peeled it off.

She couldn't stop her sharp intake of breath.

She'd thought the T-shirt had left little to the imagination, but she'd been wrong. He was quite simply magnificent, like something out of an action-adventure movie. Except he was real and apparently totally oblivious of the affect he had on her. Which was a good thing, she told herself, because she hadn't gone there to admire this man's physique.

"Look, Alex, I didn't come here to argue with you about whether I should continue practicing medicine down at the clinic."

"Why did you come, then?"

She pulled a folded check from her jeans pocket and held it out to him. "For this."

He reluctantly took the check and looked at it. "What the hell is this for?"

"It's a donation."

He thrust it back at her. "I don't need your charity."

"It's not for you." She fought the anger that rose to meet his and tossed the check on his desk. "It's for these kids and this place you've built for them."

"You think it's going to make a difference whether

you're accepted here?" Before she could answer, he went on. "You think those clothes will make a difference?"

"I . . ." She glanced down at the well-worn jeans and tank top she'd put on in an attempt to fit in.

"Take a look in the mirror, lady. Look at your skin, your hair. And if that doesn't do it, think about that car you drove in here yesterday. Most the people in this neighborhood don't see that kind of money in five years of hard work." Grabbing her check, he tore it in two. "Do us both a favor. Go ease your conscience on someone else's block."

For a moment, she couldn't speak. Then anger washed over her with dizzying intensity. "How dare you judge me." She struggled to keep her voice under control. Otherwise, she might just start screaming. "How dare you assume that you understand my motives." Though a part of her, a small niggling voice in the back of her mind, wondered if he was right. "You don't know me. You don't know the first thing about me."

"No?"

"I have as much to offer here as you."

"You forget, I grew up here."

"How could I possibly forget? You wear it on your sleeve like a badge of honor."

For a moment, he didn't respond. Then, as if they hadn't just been ready to jump down each other's throats, he said, "If you don't mind." He turned, opened a file cabinet drawer, and pulled out a clean T-shirt. Nodding toward the door she stood blocking, he added, "I need to take a shower."

She was about to tell him just how much she did mind, when someone pushed into the office behind her.

"Alejandro!"

37

Alex's attention instantly shifted, and Kristen spun around.

A small, pretty woman hurried into the room and grabbed Alex's hand. "Please. I need your help. *Es Mama.*" Then she dropped into rapid Spanish.

Kristen's Spanish needed work. She could read and write fairly well, but understanding the spoken language was another matter altogether. She picked up a few of the woman's words, enough to understand something was wrong with her mother, something physical, but mainly, Kristen heard the fear.

Alex had slipped on his shirt while they talked, and then they both started out the door.

Kristen grabbed his arm. "What's wrong?"

"I don't have time—"

"She may need a doctor. Let me help."

"No doctors," the woman said. "She won't let a doctor near her."

"She's very old," Alex added, as if that explained everything.

"Alex, don't be foolish. If she's really sick or hurt, you may need me," Kristen insisted. She looked to the distraught woman. "If not, I'll leave. I promise."

Alex hesitated and glanced at the woman. "Luisa?"

She nodded. "Please. Just come."

"Okay," he said as he turned back to Kristen. "Come if you want. But stay out of the way."

Kristen stopped only long enough to grab her medical bag from the trunk of her car before hurrying after Alex and Luisa.

The house was several blocks away, and, like the others in the neighborhood, it had seen better days. They found Luisa's mother sitting in the Florida room at the back of the house, a shawl draped across her shoulders. The shades had been drawn against the worst of the heat, but the room was still stifling.

"Mama?" Luisa went to the old woman and touched her shoulder. "I brought Alejandro to look at your arm."

The woman looked at her daughter, and then glanced at Alex before settling her gaze on Kristen.

"It's okay, Elena," he said, squatting on his heels in front of her. "This is Kristen. She's a friend and won't hurt you." When Elena looked back at him, he added, "Can I see your arm?"

After a moment's hesitation she removed the shawl to reveal her right hand resting on a bag of ice.

Alex took her wrist and turned it over, and Kristen moved closer. Climbing up the inside of the old woman's arm was a painful-looking burn, red with blisters. But that wasn't the only thing that concerned Kristen; it was the way Elena held her hand, folded in on itself as if grabbing on to something.

Kristen knelt down beside Alex. "Ask her if I can examine her arm."

When Alex didn't respond, she glanced at him and saw the doubt etched in his features.

"Ask her," Kristen insisted, turning back to meet and hold older woman's gaze. "Tell her I won't hurt her. And I promise not to do anything she doesn't like. But I can help, both with the burn and the pain in her hands."

After a moment, Alex said, "Tell her yourself. She understands English."

Kristen smiled at the old woman. Since both Alex and Luisa had used English, she'd known Elena understood as well. But Kristen had wanted to speak through one of them first out of respect. Now that he'd given her the go-ahead, she said, "May I call you Elena?"

After a moment the other woman nodded. "*Si.*"

"Will you let me look?" Kristen held out her hand.

For several seconds, Elena didn't answer. Finally, she nodded again.

Reluctantly, Alex stood and backed away, letting Kristen inch closer. He knew he had no choice but to let her examine Elena, but it bothered him. Kristen was a doctor, and that arm obviously needed medical attention. To deny her request to help would have been foolish, and he had to admit, there had been more to his decision. There was something in Kristen's eyes that convinced him—not pity, as he would have expected—but compassion and competence.

Still, Elena was an old woman. And very dear. He didn't want to see her hurt. Someone like Kristen Helton—here for a while before she returned to wherever she'd come from . . . who knew how much damage she could cause? Unfortunately, at the moment, he had no choice.

He wrapped an arm around Luisa's shoulders and watched Kristen. There was a gentleness to her touch he could see, and he wondered if she was good at doctoring. She certainly looked like she knew what she was doing.

When she spoke, it was directly to Elena. "How did you burn yourself?"

"I was making lunch. The pot slipped."

"Because of the pain in your hands?"

Elena nodded.

"You have a second-degree burn," Kristen said. "I can treat it with an ointment and give you something so it won't get infected. As for the pain . . . it's not just in your hands, is it? It's all over, in all your joints."

Elena visibly hesitated, and then nodded again.

"You have a condition called degenerative arthritis. It's common in older people and can't be cured. But I can help. I can give you something to ease the pain."

As he'd expected, Elena looked doubtful, wary even.

"The pills won't make you drowsy or sleepy," Kristen said. "I promise."

Elena seemed reluctant to agree.

It didn't stop Kristen. "I can help you," she said. "*If* you'll help me."

Surprised, Alex tensed, ready to ask her what her game was.

Elena, however, beat him to the punch. "What do you want?"

"I want to learn Spanish," Kristen said evenly, as if discussing a business transaction. "I can read and write some, but I don't understand the spoken language very well. It puts me at a disadvantage at the clinic where I work. I need someone like you to help me."

Alex held his breath for several moments, not knowing what to think. If asked, he could have come up with a number of scenarios, including Elena refusing all treatment, or Kristen offering to pay for everything. He never would have thought she'd suggest an exchange of services.

"I can teach you," Elena said finally.

"Good." Kristen reached into her bag for her supplies.

More than a little amazed, Alex watched as Kristen treated and wrapped Elena's burn and then gave her several small vials of pills. Elena examined each item Kristen gave her and listened to the instructions.

When she was all done, Kristen said, "Do you have any questions?"

"No."

"Good. Now, when can we start the lessons?"

Elena smiled, just a bit. "*Mañana.*"

Kristen laughed and stood. "Tomorrow it is."

"Don't forget."

"No, I won't." Kristen smiled at Elena and then at Alex and Luisa as she headed back toward the front of the house.

In the living room Luisa said, "I can't believe it. She actually let you help her."

"No one used the 'D' word." Grinning, Kristen was obviously pleased with herself.

Luisa laughed, but Alex wasn't so easily appeased. "Are you sure you can ease the arthritis? She's been like that for a long time."

"As I said, there's no cure," she answered. "But between the medication and my daily visits, I can work with her to get the pain under control."

"I don't think—"

Luisa interrupted him. "So, you will come every day?"

"If it's okay with you."

"Yes, please," Luisa answered.

It wasn't okay with Alex. Kristen shouldn't be alone in this house with Elena, or even Luisa, and their becoming attached to her wasn't his only concern.

Just then, the door opened, sending a stream of light into the dim room. All three of them turned toward the entry, where, standing in the doorway, was the main reason Kristen should avoid this house.

"What are they doing here?" Hector demanded.

Chapter Four

No one moved as tension slithered into the room.

Finally, Luisa started toward her son. "Hector, please . . ."

He held up both hands as if to ward her off. "Get them out of here."

"We're here to help your grandmother," Alex said, resisting the urge to put himself between the boy and his mother.

Hector turned on Alex. "Don't talk to me about helping, old man." Anger and frustration vibrated in his voice. "*You're* not welcome here."

"Hector." Luisa stepped between them. "Apologize. Now!"

"No way."

Alex fought the impulse to throttle the boy. He'd known Luisa all her life, and she didn't deserve to be treated like this—especially by her own son. Only knowing she'd probably throttle *him* for interfering kept Alex in check. Besides, she was a far cry from helpless when it came to standing up for herself.

"Where were you?" she demanded of Hector. "I have looked for you all day. Your grandmother burned herself."

A flicker of guilt touched the boy's eyes but vanished so quickly, Alex thought he might have imagined it.

"So you brought in strangers," Hector accused.

"Alejandro is no stranger." Luisa took a step closer to her son. "He belongs here as much as you."

"Oh, I forgot. *He* can do no wrong." Hector's voice held more than sarcasm, something darker, and Alex feared he'd been the one to put it there.

"Enough!" Luisa's anger rose to meet her son's. "This is my house and these are my guests. I invited them here. Now, I want you—"

Hector didn't let her finish. "What about her?" He threw an accusing look at Kristen. "Does she belong here too?"

Again, Alex started to step forward, but Luisa held out a hand to stop him, though she never took her eyes off her son.

"If you had been here, you would know why she is here. You would know that Dr. Helton came to help. But no." She threw up her hands, obviously exasperated. "You were out. Off somewhere with your friends, doing only God knows what."

"Fool woman," Hector said. "You don't know what you're talking about."

"Do not speak to me like that," she snapped, obviously at the end of her patience. "This is my house. Mine! And I asked Alejandro and the lady doctor here to help your grandmother. You owe them an apology."

Hector looked from one of them to the other, a multitude of emotions flashing across his face. Then he mumbled something in Spanish and stormed out of the house.

Alex started to follow, but Luisa grabbed his arm. "Let him go."

"Are you sure?"

She nodded. "He will be back later." With a sigh, she released Alex and turned toward Kristen. "I am sorry for what he said."

"Please"—Kristen laid a hand on Luisa's arm—"don't apologize."

Luisa pushed her heavy dark hair away from her face. "I don't know what is wrong with him. He used to be such a good boy. Strong-willed, but good."

Kristen gave Luisa an understanding smile. "Teenagers can be difficult."

"Yes," she said. "He is *difficult.*"

Alex felt her frustration as if it were his own. In a way, it was. Ever since he'd come back to the old neighborhood, he'd tried to reach the boy, not only for his sake but for Luisa's. For a while, he thought he'd succeeded. Then he'd blown it big time. Since then, Hector wanted nothing to do with him.

"I guess it is not a good idea for you to come back here," Luisa said to Kristen. "If he finds you here again, he will be very angry."

"I won't come if you don't want me to, but I'm not afraid of your son, Luisa. Maybe when he's not home—"

Luisa shook her head. "I don't know. He's usually gone during the day, but I don't know where he goes. And I never know when he is coming back."

"Luisa's right," Alex said. "I shouldn't have brought you here."

Kristen turned toward him, a challenge in her eyes. "And would you have been able to treat Elena?"

He didn't respond because they both knew the answer.

45

"She would have continued to get worse," Kristen added. "And eventually you would have had to hospitalize her."

She had a point. Still . . .

"Look"—she turned back to Luisa—"I'll keep my visits short, and we'll time them for when he's usually out. And if he does find out"—she shrugged—"he'll eventually calm down when he realizes that I'm here to help his grandmother."

"I don't know," Luisa said again, looking to Alex. "It would mean a lot to Mama. But . . ."

He wanted Luisa to refuse, but Kristen was right. This would mean a lot to Elena.

"It's up to you, Luisa," Kristen said. "But I'm willing to give it a try if you are."

"Okay," she said finally, "we can try."

* * *

Neither of them spoke as Alex and Kristen walked the few blocks from Luisa's house. It was as if they'd reached some unspoken agreement not to discuss the last hour.

That didn't mean Alex could stop his thoughts.

Kristen had surprised him in more ways than one today. First with her clothes, though he'd immediately understood what she was trying to do. Unfortunately, even in faded jeans and a T-shirt, she looked too expensive for this neighborhood.

Her winning over Luisa and Elena wasn't as easy for him to dismiss, however. Not that Luisa was a difficult conquest, but Elena had never taken to people outside her immediate circle. Kristen's request for Spanish lessons had been a stroke of genius, particularly because she'd seemed sincere and determined to carry through with it no matter what—despite Hector offering her the perfect excuse to back out.

That wasn't, however, all of it.

On top of everything else, Alex had had his doubts about Kristen's skills. Usually, the clinic ended up with doctors no one else would hire—the ones who'd graduated at the bottom of their class from some no-name medical school, or been accused of malpractice so often that no one would touch them. They'd take the job at the Hope Clinic as a last resort until something better came along.

Now, after seeing how she'd handled Elena, Alex doubted whether either scenario fit Dr. Kristen Helton. If nothing else, she knew her job.

None of which meant he understood her any more than he had a couple of hours earlier. On the contrary. She remained more of a mystery than ever.

When they arrived back at the youth center, he followed her to a small white car.

"This is it," she said.

Surprised again, Alex looked over the plain, inexpensive vehicle. It certainly wasn't what he'd expected her to drive.

"It's a rental," she explained, as if reading his thoughts.

"What about *your* car?" Though he knew the answer without asking.

"I haven't heard anything. And I don't expect to."

At least she was being realistic. "I'm sorry."

She shrugged. "As everyone pointed out, I shouldn't have driven it down here."

It would have been easy to offer some assurance that the police would find her car intact, but he wasn't going to lie to her. "I'm sure your insurance will take care of it."

"Yes, but"—she dug the keys out of her pocket—"I plan

to drive this for a while." She turned to unlock the car but stopped before opening the door. Without looking at him, she said, "Hector was the reason you didn't want me to go with you today, wasn't he?"

Alex shifted uncomfortably. "One of the reasons."

She swung around to face him. "What does he have against me?"

"You might as well ask what he has against anyone."

"Even though I'm a doctor, here to help."

"That just makes it worse." He sensed her frustration, but it was time she faced the truth. "Doctors come and go at the Hope Clinic so fast, it may as well have a revolving door. It makes it hard to believe anyone will stay more than a month or two. And the kids are often the slowest to trust once they've been burned. Hector's not any different. He's just stronger. A leader. And that makes him more dangerous."

She seemed to think about that for a moment. Finally, she asked, "What if he'd found you there alone without me?"

"Hector's not too crazy about me either."

"Because you helped me yesterday?"

He wished he could say yes, that he and Hector usually got along fine. "Yesterday just added fuel to the fire. Hector and I . . . well, let's just say we're not on the best of terms."

She nodded as if understanding, though she couldn't possibly. Still, he was grateful she didn't push further with more questions.

"Well," she said, "I guess I'd better get going."

He slipped his hands into his jeans pockets. "Yeah."

For a moment, they stood awkwardly in the fading light, the setting sun casting her hair in a fiery glow. Yesterday, she'd worn it held back with a clip. Today it floated about her shoulders, a bonfire of bright curls.

Then she smiled awkwardly and turned to open the car door.

In a flash he realized he couldn't let her go. Not without knowing why she was doing this, why she was willing to risk her life by working down here. Even temporarily.

"Why?" He made a sweeping gesture with his hand, encompassing the car, the clothes. Her.

She looked at him for a moment without answering, obviously considering her answer. Finally, she said, "I may not be able to fit in around here, but I can try not to stand out."

"That's not what I meant." He understood her driving the cheap rental—just as he understood about the clothes she'd worn today—but that wasn't what he wanted to know. "Why bother?" He stepped closer to her, as if proximity would give him the answers he sought. "What are you doing in this part of Miami? Why are you at the Hope Clinic instead of some nice, safe practice somewhere?"

"I thought you already knew the answer to that." A flicker of irritation sparked in her green eyes, confirming the myth about the fiery nature of redheads. "Didn't you say I was easing my guilty conscience?"

"Are you?" He held his ground, not backing off from his earlier statement. He still believed it, but he'd just given her a chance to deny it.

Finally, she sighed. "Look, Alex. I'm a doctor. Treating sick people is what I do. What difference does it make to you where I practice?"

But it *did* make a difference—though he couldn't for the life of him figure out why. He couldn't leave it like this. Not anymore. He needed to know more about this woman and her motives. And more than that, he needed to figure out why it mattered to him.

"Have you eaten yet?" he asked. He could tell he'd surprised her. Without giving her a chance to respond, he added, "It's getting late, and I'm starved. How about I buy you dinner? There's a little place a couple of miles from here. Nothing fancy, but the food's good."

Kristen hesitated, uncertain what to make of Alex's sudden invitation. He was a complex man who made her nervous on more levels than she cared to think about. She hardly knew him, and she certainly didn't understand him— except his work with kids. She understood that perfectly.

Feeling reckless, she said, "Sure, why not?" Although she could think of at least a half-dozen reasons why not.

None of which held any sway over her decision.

She told herself it was important to spend time with him, to win him over and gain his support if she was ever going to gain acceptance in this neighborhood. Of course, that was all just smoke. Agreeing to have dinner with him had nothing to do with practicing medicine or this neighborhood. It was about the man himself, and her resolve to get to know him better.

Another half-truth.

It was true she wanted to get to know him better, but standing just short of touching distance, she realized she wanted more than words from Alex Jamison. She wanted . .
.

She stopped herself before she could carry that crazy line of thinking any farther. Alex Jamison was totally wrong for her. Not that she was looking for a husband—or a lover for that matter—but why tempt fate, risking her heart on one and her reputation on the other?

Alex would never fit into her parents'—into *her*—world;

wanting him was dangerous. She'd learned that lesson watching what her mother had gone through over the years. Besides, he wasn't the type of man to become involved with someone like her either. A *gringa*.

She insisted on taking her own car and following him to the restaurant. It was safer than sharing the close space of the same vehicle, and it gave her time to pull in her wayward thoughts.

Unfortunately, that safety lasted only a few minutes.

He waited for her in the restaurant parking lot, darkly handsome and much too compelling for comfort.

"Have you ever eaten Cuban food?" he asked.

"No," she answered, thinking this was the perfect time to tell him she'd changed her mind about dinner. She had an early morning tomorrow at the clinic and needed her rest. But the words never came.

"Then this will be a first." He took her arm—probably an unconscious and natural gesture on his part—but she felt the heat of his touch in places best left unbreached by a man like Alex Jamison.

This was lust, pure and simple. She might as well admit it. And just because she'd never experienced it on this level before, didn't mean she had to act on it.

As they entered the small restaurant, a trim Latin woman turned and broke into a huge smile. "Alejandro!" Closing the distance between them, she threw her arms around him. "It has been months. Where have you been?"

He returned the hug with enthusiasm. "Around."

"And why haven't you been in to see me?" She backed off without releasing him. "You no longer like my cooking?"

"You know better than that." He smiled broadly. "The center keeps me busy."

"*Sí, sí,* I know. Your boys come first. This is not a bad

51

thing. But a man has to eat." Stepping out of his embrace but still holding on to his hands, she looked him up and down. "And I don't think you eat enough."

"Still trying to fatten me up?"

"It is *one* of the things a woman does for a man. And since you won't let me do the other . . ."

Kristen choked back her abrupt laughter and caught a warning glare from Alex. Fortunately, the woman picked that moment to turn toward Kristen.

"And who is this?" She jabbed Alex in the side. "A new girlfriend?"

Kristen had the distinct feeling she was being sized up.

"No," Alex answered, "this is Dr. Kristen Helton. She works down at the Hope Clinic."

"So, because she is a doctor, she can't be your girlfriend? She is pretty, classy. . . . You could do worse."

Alex laughed and shook his head. "Kristen, this is Berta, not only the neighborhood matchmaker, but the best Cuban cook in all Miami."

"It is true," she said, moving forward to take Kristen's hand. "You have never tasted Cuban food until you have eaten mine."

Kristen returned the woman's smile, liking her direct-ness and lack of false humility. "I'm looking forward to it."

"Good. Come, then." Berta escorted them to a table near the back of the room. "Sit here. You don't need menus. I will prepare some very special food tonight, just for the two of you." She patted Alex on the cheek. "Now, you want Malta or sangria?"

Alex glanced at Kristen, who shook her head, totally out of her element. "Whatever you think's best."

"Make it sangria," Alex said.

"Bueno." Nodding her approval, Berta disappeared into the kitchen.

Kristen smiled to hide her irrational twinge of jealousy toward this woman who seemed so close to Alex. "Do you know everyone in this neighborhood?"

"I grew up here."

She couldn't stop her grin. "So you've told me."

He laughed quietly. "Yeah. I guess I have."

"But you didn't stay here. You left."

"What makes you say that?"

She shrugged and leaned back in her chair. "Otherwise you wouldn't have opened the youth center. You wouldn't have understood how badly this neighborhood needed it."

Before he could respond, Berta returned and set the table with place mats, silverware, and water glasses. After she hurried off, Kristen smiled at the paper mats, complete with a map of Florida and tourist spots marked by bright red stars.

"Guess you don't see many of those where you live," Alex said.

She shook her head. "Not many." And she loved it—like everything else about the place: its simplicity and lack of pretension.

Then an old man in an immaculate white jacket brought the sangria and glasses to the table. He conversed with Alex in Spanish for a moment, then nodded and carefully placed everything in front of them.

When he left, Alex filled one of the glasses with the deep red liquid. "I was eighteen when I left," he said, taking up the conversation where they'd left off. "I'd been caught breaking into a liquor store." He set the glass in front of her while his dark gaze sought hers, as if waiting to see if he'd shocked her.

Taking her time, she sipped the fruited wine. "What happened?" she asked, keeping her voice neutral.

For a moment, he studied her without answering. "I was given a choice. Twenty-four months in the state penitentiary, or enlisting." He finally looked away, pouring a second glass of wine for himself, and she had to wonder if she'd passed his shock test. "In my mind, it was an easy decision. I chose the army."

That explained so much: his precision, his control. He was a soldier. "How long were you in?"

"Ten years. And"—he shrugged—"it saved my life. They taught me discipline and respect for the law. They even sent me to college." He laughed shortly and sipped at his drink. "Imagine, Alejandro Jamison in college."

She had no trouble picturing him as a student, a quiet, serious student. He'd have been the kind who never socialized, sat quietly in the back of the room, and consistently threw off the curve with his high test scores.

"Then one day I woke up and knew it was time to leave," he said.

"That's when you opened the youth center."

He looked down at the glass in his hand. "I wanted to start a place where kids without a stable home could get the attention and help they needed."

"Because you'd been one of those kids."

He seemed to hesitate and then lifted his shoulders in a shrug. "It's no secret. My father took off when I was eight." He leaned back in his chair. "You know the old cliché about the husband going out for a pack of cigarettes and never coming home. Well, that was my old man. Only he went out for baby aspirin. My two younger brothers and I were all sick with the flu. I guess he got tired of crying kids and the smell of vomit. He never came back."

"I'm sorry."

"Don't be." He looked irritated. "You didn't make him leave."

Kristen thought for a moment about how different their lives had been. She'd been an only child and the sole focus of a doting mother and father. Of course, it all came down to economics. Her parents had never had to deal with a sick child. There had been servants and nannies to take care of that sort of thing. And if her father had wanted out of his marriage, he wouldn't have disappeared on the way to the local drugstore. There would have been lawyers, custody battles, and financial settlements.

"Do you like the sangria?" Alex asked, drawing her out of her thoughts.

"Very much." She glanced down at the nearly full glass in her hand. "I'm just not much of a drinker."

Alex nodded, and again the silence fell around them.

Finally, Kristen said, "Did you ever see your father again?"

"Nope." Pursing his lips, Alex shook his head. "And that's probably a good thing. His leaving about killed my mother. I think I would have had to make him pay for that."

She had no doubt he could. There was a darkness in Alex she wouldn't want to cross, an underlying element of danger that would make him a formidable opponent. "Where is your mother now?"

"In a neat little condo in Jupiter."

Which Kristen figured he'd bought and paid for.

Just then, Berta and a waitress showed up, carrying a tray of fragrant food and effectively ending the conversation. With a flourish Berta placed several dishes in front of Kristen while the waitress served Alex.

"You will like this, I think," Berta said. *"Lechón, y pollo asado.* It is roast pork and roasted chicken."

"It smells wonderful," Kristen said. "And are these black beans and rice?"

"Si," Berta said, grinning. *"Arroz con frijoles negros."*

"And this is?" Kristen pointed to a side dish.

"Platanos maduros. Fried bananas. All very traditional Cuban food. Now, please," Berta said, smiling as she backed away from the table. "Enjoy your meal."

They ate for a few minutes in silence. Then Kristen said, "This is wonderful."

"It was one of the best things about coming home."

Home. Had she ever felt that way about a place? About the house and neighborhood where she'd grown up? Certainly she'd always thought of South Florida as home— the sun and beaches, the weather that seemed to fit her temperament as easily as a pair of summer shorts. But to feel drawn to a neighborhood, to people who had known you all your life, it wasn't something she'd ever experienced.

"You know," Kristen said, "most people wouldn't have come back here. Not once they'd left."

He looked at her for a moment before saying, "I had no choice." Then, he deftly changed the subject. "But what about you? Did you grow up in Miami?"

"No." She didn't really want to tell him where she *had* grown up, but she couldn't lie either. "Palm Beach."

He arched an eyebrow as if impressed. "In one of those huge mansions on the ocean?"

She felt the heat touch her cheeks. "Yes."

Obviously he'd been kidding, because he seemed a bit taken aback by her answer. "I'm sorry."

"Don't be." She put a note of sarcasm in her voice. "You didn't make me live there."

At first her response seemed to surprise him, and then he smiled. "Touché."

Kristen remembered wondering what it would take to make him smile at her. He was smiling now. His dark eyes alight with amusement—and something else. If she didn't know better, she thought it might be approval. Whatever it was, she felt the effect to her core. It seemed so absurd. She hardly knew this man and yet she felt this physical pull. Lust, she reminded herself, and something she had no intention of acting upon.

Distinctly uncomfortable, she looked away.

After a moment he said, "I didn't think the Palm Beach social set went to medical school."

"Most don't."

He grinned. "So you're an eighteen-carat rebel?"

She laughed. It was a ridiculous image—Dr. Kristen Helton, only daughter of James Helton of Palm Beach—a rebel. It made her smile. "Yeah, that's me." And she realized they had something in common. Neither of them liked talking about themselves. "Look, can we talk about something else?"

"Like what?"

She hesitated a moment, toying with the stem of her wineglass. Then she looked at him and said, "Alex, I need your help."

Chapter Five

Alex straightened, suddenly wary. "What kind of help?"

Kristen leaned forward, her green eyes lit with an intensity that stirred his senses. "Everyone in this neighborhood knows you," she said. "They trust you."

"Not necessarily." He hedged, guessing the direction she was heading and not liking it.

"Okay," she agreed. "There are exceptions. Hector, and probably a lot more who I don't know about."

Alex frowned. "Not a *lot* more."

With a flick of her wrist she brushed his comment aside. "The point is, people around here know and respect you."

He shrugged. "Maybe some."

"Okay. Some." She nodded and sat back in her chair, hesitating, as if now that she had his attention, she didn't know how to proceed. He didn't rush her. After a moment, she said, "Did you know I'm at the clinic only three and a half days a week? Monday, Wednesday, Friday, and every other Saturday."

He didn't know, but he nodded anyway.

"We keep fairly busy, but . . ." Again, she leaned forward. "I know there are others like Elena. People who, for one reason or another, won't or can't come into the clinic."

"I explained that to you."

She took a deep breath and looked down at her clasped hands. "Yes, I know." She raised her eyes back to his. "The other doctor and I, and two of the three nurses . . . none of us are from the neighborhood, and none of us have been at the clinic very long."

She'd learned a lot in a short time, he realized. But then, she'd had a crash course.

"That doesn't change the fact that I have three days a week open," she said. "I can treat these people. I *want* to treat them."

"What does that have to do with me?" Although again, he thought he knew.

"I need you to help me reach them. Take me around. Introduce me."

"You can't ask them all to teach you Spanish."

She smiled tentatively. "With your help and Elena's, I won't have to."

"How do you figure?"

"If you vouch for me, they'll accept me."

For several moments, he didn't respond. "Suppose you're right. Suppose one word from me and people would open their doors to you. Why would I want to do that?"

She seemed surprised by the question. "Why not? I'm a doctor, and I'm offering free medical care for the housebound."

"What happens when you get tired of slumming it?" It was his turn to lean forward, to pin her with his eyes. "When you decide it's time to go back to Palm Beach?

What happens then to the people who began to depend on you?"

She went very still. "First of all . . ." she started, her voice a study in controlled emotion, "slumming it is not a phrase I would use. And what makes you so sure I'm going to go running back to Palm Beach?"

"Come on, Kristen, I've seen it before. You're not the first bleeding heart we've had come into our neighborhood, trying to save us from ourselves."

"So, what happened, Alex?" She crossed her arms, her eyes flashing with anger. "Did someone tread on your over-sized toes?"

He shifted uncomfortably in his chair, realizing he'd said too much. Hell, he'd been saying too much all evening. "It doesn't matter."

Again, bright green anger flashed in her eyes. "It does if you're assuming I'm going to behave like someone else."

"No one's accusing you of anything."

"Look, Alex—" She stopped and visibly curbed her temper.

He wondered how long it had taken her to learn how to do that, because he suspected control didn't come easy for her.

"Obviously," she continued finally, "I'm not going to convince you that I won't go running back to Palm Beach. So I'm not even going to try. Besides, we both know there are no guarantees. Ever. But why not take advantage of me while I'm here?"

When he didn't answer right away, she reached across the table and placed her hand on his, and it took all his willpower to keep from snatching it away. "Alex, please, trust me."

The thing was, he wanted to trust her, wanted to believe

she would be different, that she could do some good for the people in his neighborhood. But experience held him back, made him cautious. He wasn't the only one with something at stake here. For that same reason, he couldn't offhandedly dismiss her offer either. As she'd said, she was offering free medical care for the housebound. What right did he have to turn her down?

After a moment, he pulled his hand from beneath hers. "I'll think about it."

Kristen shook her head. "I guess I can't ask for more than that."

He started to answer just as Berta and the waitress returned. "Are you ready for dessert?" Berta asked as the waitress began clearing the table.

A bit unnerved by the interruption, Alex glanced at Kristen.

"None for me," she said, smiling graciously. No one would guess that a moment earlier she'd been angry enough to leap across the table and strangle him. "But everything was wonderful, Berta. Thank you."

"Café Cubana, then?" Berta offered.

"No, thank you," Alex said. "Just the check, Berta."

It took a few minutes to convince her they were serious about not wanting anything else. Actually, Alex couldn't wait to get out of there. He needed to put a little distance between himself and Dr. Kristen Helton, to gain some perspective on her request, and to get control of his wayward reactions to the woman herself. Finally, after saying good-bye to Berta, they made their way out of the restaurant.

Outside, full darkness and a half-moon had taken hold of the sky, but the city lights kept the night at bay. The breeze off the ocean had picked up, stirring air a few degrees cooler than earlier, but it was still hot. And would be until nearly dawn.

"Do you know how to get onto the highway from here?" Alex asked as they headed toward Kristen's car.

"I think so."

A few more steps and he said, "Are you still planning on working with Elena tomorrow?" He knew it was a stupid question, but couldn't think of anything better to say.

"In the morning. About ten."

"Good." They stopped next to her car, and he wedged his hands into the back pockets of his jeans. He couldn't remember the last time he'd felt this awkward around a woman. "Are you sure you know how to get home from here?"

"Yes." She nodded without looking at him. "Thank you for dinner. It was great."

He shrugged. "No problem."

She smiled, and he searched for something else to say, something to keep her there a moment or two longer. He was reluctant to let her leave. "Well," he said, coming up blank. "Good night, then."

"Good night."

She turned to unlock her car, and he started to walk away.

He couldn't have said what made him look back, but he was only a few feet from her when the urge struck him. As if sensing him, she turned at the same moment, stopping him.

Maybe it was the moonlight, or the tropical night air drifting between them. Or maybe it was the promise he'd seen earlier in those vivid green eyes—the promise of fire. Or maybe it was simply that he wanted to test those lips, to find out for himself if they were as soft as they looked, as sweet as he imagined.

If she'd glanced away or even seemed hesitant, that would have ended it. He'd have spun on his heel and walked away from her. Instead, she met his gaze head-on, a question in her green eyes, and it broke the last of his restraint. Before he realized his intentions, he'd closed the distance between them and pulled her into his arms. Her mouth met his in a kiss as fierce as the Florida sun. Then she wrapped her arms around his neck, rising on her toes to meet him and pull her body against the full length of his.

He knew then he was in big trouble.

* * *

Nine-thirty in the morning and already a relentless sun poured heat from a cloudless sky. Sometimes Alex believed there was no place on earth hotter than Miami, and it was beginning to feel like today would be one of those days.

He took up a position under the overgrown banyan across from the Hope Medical Clinic and waited. He had about a half hour before Kristen was due to make the trip to see Elena, but he hadn't wanted to take a chance on missing her. Not with tempers in the neighborhood rising to meet the mid-August heat.

Unfortunately, waiting gave him too much time to think.

Scrutinizing the previous day's events, he tried to figure out where he'd gone wrong. What he could have done differently to change the way it had ended.

With the kiss.

Going as far back as Luisa's request for help, he could have changed things. He could have refused to take Kristen along, but as she'd pointed out, who would have treated Elena? He'd stopped in to check on her earlier this morning, and from the way she'd snapped at him, he knew she was already feeling better. So he couldn't regret taking Kristen to see the older woman.

Probably, then, he shouldn't have asked Kristen to dinner—though at the time it had seemed like a good idea. Except that nothing about the evening had gone according to plan.

He'd intended to rid himself of the mystery surrounding her, to understand her motives and thus free himself from thinking about her, wondering about her. He'd expected to confirm his initial suspicions and discover a spoiled rich woman on a mission to ease her conscience. Instead, he'd enjoyed her company, finding her intelligent and determined, with a hidden fire he wanted to explore. Hell, he'd even ended up talking about himself—something he very seldom did.

Not that he'd told her anything she couldn't have found out on the nearest street corner. Like in a small town, secrets were difficult to keep in this neighborhood. *His* past in particular seemed grist for the local gossip mill.

Still, if he'd left it at that, everything would have been fine. If only he hadn't kissed her.

He could have spent the rest of his life wondering, fantasizing even, about the taste of those lips. Now he knew, and they'd been sweeter than anything he could have imagined. He was setting himself up for a fall. She made him want things he couldn't have, a woman so far out of his reach, he could easier reach for the sun.

Unfortunately, knowledge didn't stop the wanting.

* * *

Kristen had learned in medical school how to function on small amounts of sleep. So that wasn't the problem. She could work even though she'd tossed and turned all night. But nothing had prepared her to deal with the memories from the night before. They stole her focus and left her feeling one step behind everyone else.

Luckily, things were slow at the clinic. The nurse-receptionist confirmed that Wednesdays were usually their lightest day, with things picking up toward the weekend. Otherwise, Kristen might not have made it through the morning.

More than once she found herself reliving Alex's kiss. She recalled how his hands had felt on her back, the restless way they'd moved up and down her spine, drawing her against the hard lines of his body, his arousal pressed against her lower belly. And, if she closed her eyes, she imagined she could still taste him, feel the contours of his mouth, the pressure of his lips, the thrust and parry of his tongue. Now, hours later, just the thought of his kiss had the power to make her tremble.

No man had ever kissed her like that before, with a need that both stole her breath and demanded her response. Nor had she ever reacted with such abandon. During those few minutes in his arms, she'd wanted him desperately. All of him. If he'd dragged her into the backseat of her car, she would have gone willingly, eagerly.

Fortunately, *he'd* come to his senses, releasing her almost as abruptly as he'd taken hold of her. She might have been offended, but she'd felt the strength of his desire and knew a certain amount of feminine thrill in having that kind of power. He was a man of control and precision, and the intensity of the chemistry between them had thrown him as much as her.

As the morning wore on, she tried reminding herself of the reasons she shouldn't become involved with Alex. But her mind was blank. After all, she wasn't planning to marry the man. Why couldn't they enjoy each other until the chemistry between them fizzled out?

Unfortunately, that wasn't an option. Not for her.

While in medical school, she'd become involved with one of her professors. Despite the strict rules against it, she'd let him convince her no one would ever know, that there would be no repercussions. He'd been wrong. Although he'd kept his word, and their affair remained a secret, when she'd tried to break things off, he'd made life hell for her.

Things could easily become that complicated with Alex.

As long as she stayed at the Hope Clinic, they'd be crossing paths, and if he agreed to help her gain the neighborhood's trust, they'd be working together. She couldn't risk destroying that potential relationship for a brief affair. No matter how tempting.

Just then, her cell phone buzzed and her mother's name popped up on the screen. Kristen closed the medical journal she'd been attempting to read and picked up the phone. "Hello, Mother." Smiling, Kristen rose and closed the door to her small office. "How are you?"

"Fine, dear. I hope I haven't caught you at an inconvenient time. I know how busy you are."

Kristen glanced at her watch. "Actually, this is a good time." It would get her mind off Alex. "I have to go out around ten, but I have a few minutes."

"Good. Tell me, how are things going down there? I've been thinking about you."

Kristen thought of everything that had happened in the past couple of days: her stolen car, her run-ins with Hector, meeting Alex, kissing him . . . "I ate Cuban food last night for the first time," she said. "It was delicious."

"I do hope you were careful."

"Careful?"

"Well, I know the neighborhoods down there can be pretty rough."

"Yes, Mother, I was careful." So much for telling her about Hector or Alex.

"Have you settled into the apartment?"

"Yes, pretty much."

"You know, if you'd rather have a house—"

"The condominium is more than adequate."

Talking to her mother was often like this, an exchange of pleasantries with no substance. Kristen wished they could have a real conversation for once. She would have liked to tell someone about Alex and her mixed feelings about him. Who more appropriate than her mother? Unfortunately, Kristen knew how her mother would react if she mentioned her interest in a man like Alex Jamison, a man from the streets of Miami. Her mother had learned her lesson, even if Kristen hadn't.

"And the clinic?" Carolyn asked, and Kristen realized this was the main reason for her mother's call.

"Why don't you come down and see for yourself?"

"Oh, I don't know . . ."

"Better yet," Kristen said, thinking it wouldn't help her situation in the neighborhood if her mother showed up in her usual style—complete with limousine and driver. "Why don't I come up and get you on one of my days off?"

"I don't think your father would approve." Kristen heard the longing in her mother's voice.

"Don't tell him."

Carolyn hesitated. "I couldn't do that."

Of course, that was the problem. Her mother wouldn't go against James Helton's wishes. Not that he was overly demanding, just a bit stiff in his ways. In his mind, the Hope Medical Clinic wasn't the kind of place for either his wife or daughter.

Kristen considered pushing her mother a little harder, but decided against it. She'd been down this road with her mother before and knew she would never oppose her father.

"There was another reason I called this morning," Carolyn said. "Your father's birthday is coming up."

Kristen mentally groaned.

"It's his sixtieth," her mother said quickly, as if guessing Kristen's reaction. "And I want this to be a particularly special party. You'll come up, won't you?"

"Mother . . ." She knew how much Kristen hated these things—the extravagant parties with the overly dressed guest list, and no doubt a prospective husband or two. She'd have much preferred an intimate family get-together, but that wasn't going to happen. At least not for her father's birthday. It was a yearly event attended by the better part of Palm Beach's elite.

Maybe she could take Alex. She almost laughed aloud at the ridiculous notion. Wouldn't that set things on end?

"It would mean so much to him," her mother said. "To both of us."

Kristen hesitated, although she knew there was no point. She wouldn't leave her mother to fend off the vultures on her own. "Of course I'll come."

"I'm so pleased. I'll send down Thomas to pick you up."

"That's okay. I'll drive myself."

"Oh, Kristen . . ."

"Don't worry, Mother. I'll get a car and driver."

She thought again about Alex and taking him to meet

her family. A stupid idea. Like a slap in the face, it reminded her of all the reasons she shouldn't get involved with him.

* * *

A few minutes later, Kristen stepped out into the bright morning sunlight, the warmth of the day wrapping itself around her like a caress. Then she spotted Alex. He stood across the street, leaning against the trunk of an ancient banyan tree, looking unforgivably sexy in denim and a sky-blue T-shirt.

What was it about this man that set her heart racing?

A stupid question, she realized. He had a body to die for, he kissed like a demon, and, like any other red-blooded woman, she responded.

He crossed the street, closing the distance between them.

Giving him what she hoped was a normal smile and not a silly grin, she said, "Good morning, Alex."

He nodded, his expression dark and unyielding. "Dr. Helton."

She wouldn't let his somber mood ruin her delight in this day. In seeing him again. Especially when she thought that mood might have something to do with her and the kiss they'd shared last night. "Dr. Helton? We're back to that again?"

"It's probably safer."

"You have a point." Still grinning, she turned and started down the street, and he fell into step beside her. "I don't suppose you're going to tell me what you're doing here."

"Same thing as you."

She glanced at him, unable to resist the urge to tease him just a little. "Really? Your Spanish needs work as well?"

"I need to see Luisa. Since we're going in the same direction—" He stopped in mid-sentence and shook his head. "The hell with it. The truth is, I need to go with you today. In case Hector shows up."

She couldn't help but smile. "Thank you." Then, because she didn't want to burden him or anyone else, she said, "But it's really not necessary. I'll be fine."

"I'm not doing it for you. I'm doing it for Luisa and Elena."

"Of course," she said, unable to hold on to her smile.

"Look, I'm sorry, that came out wrong."

"You don't need to apologize." What did she think? One kiss, and suddenly this man was on her side, believing in her? Lust, she reminded herself, that's all there was between them. "I know your first priority is to the people of this neighborhood."

Alex mentally kicked himself. He hadn't meant to sound so blunt. It was just that from the moment she'd stepped out of the clinic, he'd felt himself drawn further under her spell. And he hated it. She made him want things he couldn't have. She'd looked so young and fresh, her hair like a flame in the sunlight, her pleasure at seeing him lighting her face. He'd wanted nothing more than to draw her into his arms and reacquaint himself with her honeyed lips.

He'd just barely resisted.

It was a mistake to want her. This attraction between them would lead nowhere, and if they weren't careful, it could destroy them both. But there was something else he could do for her, something she wanted from him.

"About last night," he started to say. "I'm sorry I—"

"Don't worry about it," she said, cutting him off. "It never happened."

"You've changed your mind about treating shut-ins?"

She flushed crimson, and he stopped abruptly, grabbing her arm and turning her to face him. "What did you think I was going to say?" he asked.

"Nothing." She pulled free of his hold and started to move away. "Never mind."

"Like hell." He stopped her again. "You thought I was going to apologize for kissing you."

"No, I . . ."

He touched her cheek. He had no choice, the blush of color against her pale skin drew him, reminded him of the hidden heat he'd had a brief taste of. "I'm not going to apologize for wanting you."

She took a deep breath and lifted her expressive green eyes to his. "It's probably best that we both forget about it."

"Maybe. But that doesn't mean I'm sorry it happened, or that I *can* forget."

For a breathless moment, she didn't reply. Then she said, "Me either."

He almost kissed her again. Right there in the middle of the block, halfway between the Hope Clinic and his youth center. Only, he knew if he did, he might not be able to stop. Then it would be all over the neighborhood within hours that Alejandro Jamison had fallen hard for the new lady doctor. Wouldn't that get a few laughs.

As if by silent consensus, they turned and started walking again. "You're right," he said after a moment. "This can't go anywhere."

"No, it can't."

"We're too different." He shook his head, not quite

believing he was having this conversation. "Hell, you're from Palm Beach of all places."

"Yes."

They walked on a bit farther. "So what do you suggest?" he asked.

At first, she didn't answer. Finally, she said, "Maybe the best thing would be if we stay out of each other's way."

Out of sight, out of mind? "That might work." Though he doubted it. "Except for one thing. You need me to get acceptance in the neighborhood."

She threw him a quick glance.

"I've thought of a few people I can introduce you to. People who might need medical care."

This time she stopped. "When?"

She seemed to have forgotten all about the problem between them, and it irritated him. "Tomorrow?"

"Why not this afternoon? We're slow at the clinic—"

"I can't. I have things to do."

The center's computer equipment was years out of date, and he wanted his kids to have the advantage of using the latest educational and graphic software. Tonight, he had an appointment with Sal and a ten-thousand-dollar purse. He figured with a little bargaining, that should cover several high-end laptops and a few notebooks and still leave some money left in the accounts for emergencies. "Tomorrow will have to be soon enough."

After the briefest pause, she nodded. "Okay."

"You're a dangerous woman, Kristen Helton." She started to say something, but he stopped her. "You have no idea how dangerous.

"What you're offering these people is hope. It's a wonderful gift. While it lasts. But it can devastate when it's taken away, which will happen if you decide to up and leave."

"Then why are you helping me?"

"Because you can do a lot of good too."

"What about you, Alex? How do you fit into all this?"

He felt the pull of her and the promise in those deep green eyes. "I'm more at risk than anybody."

Chapter Six

As they walked the last few blocks to Elena's house, Alex's words circled in Kristen's head. The things he'd said, and what he hadn't. Obviously, the chemistry between them disturbed him as much as it did her. Maybe more. And why not? She was as much an outsider in his world as he would be in hers. He'd promised to help her because of the medical care she could provide, and they'd agreed to ignore this physical attraction neither of them wanted.

Yet the memory of his kiss, his touch, still lingered.

The problem was circular with no easy solution. She needed time to think, to put things in perspective. She needed to get away from Alex so she could forget how much she wanted him to kiss her again.

When they arrived at Elena's, Alex stayed outside and Kristen went in alone. Luisa had gone to work, and Elena was waiting, feeling better and obviously eager to start on their first Spanish lesson.

For the first time all day, Kristen managed to put aside her thoughts of Alex. From the moment she stepped into the house, the older woman refused to speak or understand English. At first, Kristen found it frustrating, irritating even, but then she began to appreciate Elena's strategy. She wasn't being ornery; she was teaching Kristen the spoken language.

An hour later, as Alex walked her back to the clinic, she felt a renewed sense of hope. Despite the potential problems between Alex and her, she was doing good work here. She'd treated Elena and was learning Spanish.

Back at the clinic, it was as if the universe understood her need for mental respite and granted her wish. The normal slow Wednesday traffic picked up, and she spent the rest of the day doing what she did best, treating patients—without a moment to spare for thinking about Alex Jamison and how good it had felt to be held in his arms.

* * *

Her optimism lasted until the next morning when she arrived at the youth center. Everything was quiet, and she wondered where the boys spent their time on a hot summer day. She found LJ in the office, poring over what looked like a ledger.

She tapped lightly on the door frame. "Good morning, LJ."

He looked up and smiled broadly. "Morning, Doc."

She laughed softly. "Doc?"

"It fits you."

"Funny, I always pictured Doc as a short, white-haired country doctor. Usually male."

"Looks like you're wrong on all counts."

She laughed again, LJ's good humor infectious. "I'm supposed to meet Alex around ten. Is he here?"

LJ shook his head. "Sorry, he couldn't make it. I'm afraid you're stuck with me."

"Is something wrong?"

"Not that I know of." Although something in his eyes made her think he wasn't as unconcerned as he wanted her to believe. "He called this morning and told me he was going to be tied up. Asked me to take you over and introduce you to Ana."

She tried to hide her disappointment. "Ana?"

"She's about four months pregnant and hasn't been to see a doctor. I'd say finances were the problem, but she could go down to the clinic if she wanted. The thing is, she's got five other kids and doesn't get out much. Her oldest son spends some time here, so Alex thought she'd be a good place to start."

"It sounds like he's right." She had to keep her priorities straight. It didn't matter *who* took her to meet this woman, just that she was able to reach someone who needed her help.

"Just give me a minute to finish up here"—he motioned toward the ledger—"and we'll get going."

"No hurry." Kristen wandered out into the center's main room.

Alex had solved the problem. He'd given her what she wanted, a chance to work in the neighborhood without constantly worrying about the attraction between the two of them. He would set up the meetings, and LJ would make the introductions. It was a great solution.

Then why did she feel like she'd just been dumped?

The meeting with Ana went well. Kristen arranged maternity supplements and set up a schedule to check on the woman's progress.

On the way back to the center, LJ kept her laughing

with stories about his and Alex's days in the military. It was a whole different side of Alex, a lighter, more humorous side that she'd only caught glimpses of when he was around his boys.

Circling the building, they went to the side entrance. A white van stood near the door, and Kristen had to suppress her automatic reaction at the sight of Alex's powerful bare back lifting a stack of boxes from the van.

Then he turned toward them, and she saw the white tape covering his chest.

* * *

Alex ached.

It felt as if every muscle and joint in his body had been traumatized. It had been a close call last night. For a few minutes, he thought he'd lost. He'd actually seen his chance at obtaining new computers for the center slip through his fists. The image had jarred him, giving him the strength to turn the tide. He'd pushed himself to the limit and walked away with ten thousand in cash.

He could have spent the entire day in bed—probably should have. The medic who'd treated his bruised rib and sprained wrist had recommended he take it easy for a few days. But Alex had things to do. He couldn't afford to lie around, waiting to mend. After asking LJ to take care of Kristen that morning, he'd headed out to get the new laptops and notebooks for the center. Top of the line.

He should have realized Kristen and LJ would be arriving back at any time. He should have at least kept his shirt on—it would have disguised most of the damage—but he hadn't done either. He'd been eager to get the systems up and running, and with the August heat and humidity in full force, he'd taken off his shirt to unload the van.

And he'd gotten caught.

Arms weighed down by the stack of boxes, he turned as they walked into the yard and realized his mistake the instant he spotted Kristen.

She closed the distance between them in record time. "What happened to you?" She reached out and touched his taped ribs.

He flinched involuntarily.

"You shouldn't be carrying that," she said. "LJ, come get this."

Alex cursed under his breath as LJ appeared at his side.

"What have you got here, Alex?" he asked, an undercurrent of disapproval in his voice.

Alex ignored it. "The new laptops we talked about."

LJ frowned but moved to relieve Alex of his load. "Here, let me take it."

Alex relinquished boxes but turned to retrieve others from the van.

"What are you doing?" Kristen demanded. "Let LJ get that."

He grabbed the boxes and slid the van door shut with a little more force than necessary. "LJ's got his arms full." He started toward the door. She followed, not saying anything, but he felt her watching him, taking in the Ace bandage on his wrist and the cut above his left eye.

"Okay," she said as he put down his load inside. "Let me take a look at you."

Alex grabbed his shirt and slipped it on. "I've already had someone take care of it."

"What happened?" LJ demanded.

"It was nothing." Alex cursed himself for getting into

this situation. As always, his timing was just great. A half hour earlier or later, and he'd have had only LJ to deal with.

"Nothing?" Kristen sounded incredulous. "You look like you've been in a fight."

Think fast, Jamison. Something they'll both believe. He almost laughed aloud. Right. A doctor and an ex-Army Ranger. Telling them he ran into a door wouldn't cut it.

"Okay," he said, figuring he'd stick as close to the truth as possible. "I had a run-in with a pretty nasty character last night. He'd had too much to drink. He took a few swings, and so did I."

Kristen looked like she didn't know whether to believe him or not. And LJ? Hell, Alex had about given up trying to read the other man's poker face years ago.

"If it makes you feel better," Alex added, "the other guy is in worse shape than I am."

"Let me look at it." She reached out to touch him again, and he grabbed her wrist.

"I said, it's already been taken care of."

She snatched back her hand, rubbing at her wrist.

"Look . . ." he said, feeling like a heel. He hadn't meant to bark at her and touching her was never a good idea. "I'm okay. Really. It was nothing. Just a friendly brawl that got out of hand." He glanced from her to LJ and saw the sharp disapproval in his friend's eyes. So much for his poker face.

Time to change the subject.

"Why don't you tell me how things went with Ana." He looked expectantly from Kristen to LJ and back to Kristen again. Neither of them seemed inclined to answer.

Finally, she said, "It went fine. Thank you for setting it up."

"You're welcome." He forced a smile, trying to dispel the somber mood in the room. It didn't work.

"I know of one other person who might see you, but I'll have to talk to him first. He's a full-blown shut-in."

Kristen nodded, visibly distancing herself. "I'd appreciate it."

"No problem. I'll let you know when I've talked to him."

"Sure, that'll be fine. Well, if there's nothing else, I'd better get going. Thanks for taking me to Ana's, LJ." She gave him a half-smile before turning back to Alex. She glanced at his now-covered chest before lifting her gaze to his. She seemed reluctant to leave. "If you change your mind about letting someone look at you . . ."

She didn't finish her sentence, but something inside him shifted at her words, at their implication. Despite his brusque behavior, she would help him, treat his injuries if he let her. It made him understand what she'd been trying to tell him since they'd first met.

Kristen Helton cared.

Her background and upbringing didn't matter. This woman was first and foremost a healer; caring for the sick and injured was more than what she did. It was *who* she was.

The realization left him shaken and uneasy as he watched her walk out the door. He had the sudden urge to call her back, but then he felt LJ's eyes on his back and realized he couldn't afford the luxury. Best to just let her go.

Things had been strained between him and LJ for the past few months, and Alex regretted that. But he didn't know what he could do about it. Telling LJ the truth would only make things worse. He might understand. Then again, he might not.

Alex braced himself for the questions. The accusations.

LJ didn't disappoint him. "Where did you get the money for those laptops?"

"We've been over this before." Alex turned and started toward his office. "And I still don't want to talk about it."

LJ followed. "Looks to me like you bruised a couple of ribs. Or cracked them maybe."

"Leave it alone."

"Can't do that. So stop bullshitting me and tell me the truth."

Alex spun around. "Are you calling me a liar?"

"What I'm saying"—LJ took a step toward him—"is that whole story you told Kristen was a crock. And those bad ribs of yours are somehow related to those brand-new laptops and notebooks." He paused to let his words sink in. "So, as I said before, how about the truth for a change?"

Alex couldn't answer, couldn't utter another lie. Instead, he stood trying to steel himself against the anger and betrayal in his friend's eyes.

"Just tell me if what you're doing is illegal," LJ said. "Because if it is, I'm out of here, man. These kids don't deserve that."

Alex sighed and backed away, lowering himself carefully into a nearby chair. He could give LJ this much of the truth. "I'm not breaking any laws." *Except a few of my own.* "I swear."

LJ visibly hesitated, and Alex realized he'd lost this man's trust.

"You know," LJ said finally, "Langford is just itching to pin something on you and shut us down."

"I know." Suddenly, Alex felt very tired. "But he can't touch me."

"Let's hope so, my friend. Because these kids here"—he

made a sweeping gesture with his arm—"they look up to you. They *believe* in you. I'd hate to see you let them down."

"Me too, LJ. Me too."

* * *

Kristen couldn't go home. Not yet. It would give her too much time to think, to fume about Alex. He'd made her angry. At the same time, she was worried about him. Knowing she had no right to either emotion only irritated her further.

He owed her nothing.

The one thing he'd promised—to introduce her to some of the people in the neighborhood—he'd done. She couldn't fault him for asking LJ to go with her. Nor could she expect him to let her act as his doctor.

She didn't buy the barroom-brawl story, and neither had LJ. Not that she didn't think Alex capable of getting into a fight. In this case, it just didn't ring true. There was something else going on, something he wasn't telling them. And it worried her.

The whole thing left her angry, confused, and very much aware of how little she knew about him. All of which reinforced her feelings that getting involved with Alex Jamison, on any level, would be a mistake.

Too bad only her head was listening.

She went down to the clinic to see if they needed an extra pair of hands. Fortunately for her, they did. The day had brought a rash of summer colds and flu. Kristen, grateful for any kind of distraction, jumped in to help. It kept her busy and her mind off Alex.

She ended up staying late. The nurse who usually shut down the facility had been feeling poorly all day, so Kristen sent her home early and agreed to close up. It was dark by the time she left, and as she started to lock the front door, she heard footsteps come up behind her.

Startled, she spun around. "Who's there?"

"Sorry," said a vaguely familiar male voice. "Did I frighten you, Dr. Helton?" He moved into the light, a smile on his face.

"Detective Langford." Her heartbeat gradually returned to normal. "I guess my mind was somewhere else."

"Not a good idea in this neighborhood."

"So I've learned." She finished locking the door and turned back to him. "Were you looking for me or just out strolling?"

"May I walk you to the parking lot?"

"Sure." Kristen started down the sidewalk, and he fell into step beside her. After a moment she asked, "Have you heard anything about my car, Detective?"

"Please," he said, "call me Frank."

Kristen glanced at him, and again he flashed her that smile. He really was a handsome man, blond, blue-eyed, the all-American boy next door. "Okay, Frank."

"Unfortunately," he said, "we haven't found out anything about your car."

"You don't expect to, do you?"

He shook his head. "I'm sorry."

"Well, all of you were right. I should never have brought that car down here."

He didn't respond, and she thought how different he seemed from the pushy man she'd met earlier in the week. Tonight, he was easygoing and amicable. It made her wonder which persona was the real Frank Langford.

They arrived at the parking lot, and she led the way to

her car. He looked it over, much as Alex had done, and nodded in approval.

"A rental," he said. "Good idea."

"I try not to make the same mistake twice."

"Look," he said, "is there somewhere we can go and have a cup of coffee or something?"

"I really don't think—"

"Please, Dr. Helton, I know we got off to a shaky start the other night. That was my fault, and I apologize. But I have some questions I'd like to ask you. And," he said, glancing around at the seemingly quiet neighborhood, "I don't think this is the right place."

"Questions?" She crossed her arms. "Official questions?"

"Not exactly. Although they do pertain to an ongoing investigation. Please, just a half hour of your time." He smiled. "My treat."

Kristen wanted to know what kind of questions he could possibly ask her. Plus, she admitted to a certain amount of curiosity about the man and his relationship to Alex.

"Okay, Detective, let's go."

She followed him to an all-night diner. Inside, he picked a booth near the back and ordered coffee for both of them.

While they waited, Kristen studied him, comparing him to Alex. It was hard to believe they'd grown up in similar circumstances, that at one time they'd been rivals. No, actually that piece wasn't hard to believe. They were complete opposites. Not just physically but in every other discernible way: choice of profession, temperament, even their clothing choices. But what struck her the most was that while Alex clung to his old neighborhood, trying to improve it by working with its youth, Frank Langford seemed intent on shaking free of it.

Once the waitress brought their coffee, Kristen decided she didn't want to waste any more time. "So, what are these questions you want to ask me?"

He took his time answering, pouring cream into his coffee and stirring it. "I ran a background check on you."

Kristen bristled, but before she could voice her objections, he held up a hand to stop her. "Please, don't be angry. It's standard procedure under these circumstances."

"What circumstances? My car being stolen?"

"It has nothing to do with you or your car."

"Then why bring me here to ask questions?" She leaned forward, resting her arms on the tabletop. "And why check up on me?"

"As I mentioned earlier, I'm involved in an ongoing investigation." He shrugged. "And you are an unknown."

"What kind of investigation?"

He took a deep breath and looked appropriately embarrassed. "I can't tell you that."

Her frustration grew, but she kept it in check. "Okay, so you checked up on me. I assume you discovered my secret. I'm a career criminal who's been evading the law for years."

He laughed. "On the contrary, Dr. Helton . . . Kristen" —he flashed that brilliant smile—"you've led an exemplary life. Top of your class at Duke, then on to Harvard Medical School, where you graduated in the top five percent. Impressive."

She didn't bother to acknowledge the compliment, just waited to see where this was headed.

"The only thing I don't understand," he said, frowning, "is why you're here."

She would have left right then if not for her curiosity. "Is that what you brought me here to ask? Because if it—"

Again, he held up a hand and cut her off. "I'm sorry. No. That was a strictly personal question. My own curiosity."

Kristen nodded, not really appeased. She was getting awfully tired of that particular question and that no one listened to her answer.

"What I really wanted to ask you is . . ." He seemed to hesitate, as if trying to come up with the right way to phrase the question. "Have you noticed anything unusual at the clinic lately?"

"Unusual?" She crossed her arms. "I'm afraid you're going to have to be more specific than that, Detective."

"Oh, I don't know." He shrugged casually and leaned back in the booth. "Missing equipment. Unusual prescriptions. Missing drugs."

"Drugs?" As the newest doctor at the clinic, Kristen had been assigned the duty of the daily drug count. She knew there were no drugs missing but decided to play along and see where he was going with this. "Why? Do you suspect someone of stealing drugs from the clinic?"

He lifted his hands, but Kristen beat him to the punch. "I know," she said, "you can't tell me."

He smiled, obviously pleased she was such a quick study.

"No," she said. "I haven't noticed anything unusual at the clinic. Nothing 'missing,' as you say. However, I've been there only a week. Maybe you should talk to one of the other doctors. Or one of the nurses."

"Good idea," he said as if the idea hadn't occurred to him. Then, leaning forward, he sipped his coffee.

Kristen waited. He wasn't done, and she didn't think this conversation was about the clinic, missing drugs or not.

"How much do you know about Alex Jamison?" he asked suddenly.

The question should have surprised her. The fact that it didn't testified to what she'd suspected all along. Frank Langford wanted to know about Alex. The question about missing equipment and drugs had been a smoke screen to get information about him—as if she had any. She thought of his taped ribs and wrapped wrist, and his story about a barroom fight. And about the new laptops, and LJ's obvious displeasure over them.

"Not much," she answered. "He runs the youth center down the street from the Hope Clinic. And from what I can tell, he's devoted to his boys. People in the neighborhood think he's a saint."

"Yes. It would appear that way."

She wanted to believe this man's questions meant nothing, just a continuation of his animosity toward Alex. But it was hard. She'd felt the inherent danger in Alex, and Frank was a police officer. And there were the new laptops . . .

"Is Alex Jamison the subject of this *ongoing* investigation?" she asked.

"I'm afraid I can't answer that."

"Of course not."

He hesitated a moment, toying with his coffee cup. "Kristen, I'd like to give you some advice, if you don't mind."

"Can I stop you?"

He grinned, looking embarrassed. "I guess I deserve that. But this is for your own good." He paused again. "Stay away from Jamison."

"Really, I hardly know—"

"He's a very dangerous man. And I'd hate to see you hurt."

"I'll remember that." She gathered up her purse. "Now, if those are all of your questions, it's getting late and I've had a very long day."

"Of course." Tossing a couple of bills on the table, he picked up the check and slid from the booth.

Kristen went outside as he paid the bill. A light rain had fallen while they were inside, leaving the air cooler than earlier. Still, the humidity hung in the air, thick and oppressive.

He joined her a few minutes later.

"What is it between you and Alex, Detective?" she asked, throwing caution to the wind.

"What do you mean?"

"You know what I mean. You and Alex obviously don't have warm feelings for each other."

He hesitated a moment and then said, "I probably know Jamison better than anyone around here. In fact, I may be the only one who really knows him."

"How's that?"

Again, he hesitated and glanced away. When he looked back at her, he pinned her with an expression that had lost all trace of its earlier warmth. "Alex Jamison killed my brother."

Chapter Seven

Alex glanced at his watch. Almost midnight.

He'd spent most of the afternoon getting the new equipment up and running. Then the boys had started filtering in around three. Their excitement about the laptops made everything Alex had done to get them worthwhile, and helping the kids had kept him busy for the rest of the evening.

Otherwise, he might have gone after Kristen.

He'd thought about it enough, in between hooking up printers, getting everyone online, and downloading software. Even while he was working with the boys, the idea had crept into his consciousness. He didn't know why or what he'd say to her. He just knew he wanted to go after her and . . . what? Apologize? Explain how he'd managed to bruise two ribs and sprain his wrist?

Get real, Jamison!

A woman like Kristen Helton would run for the hills if she discovered the truth. It was better to leave things alone and let her imagine whatever she would.

So the day had worn on until the boys started heading

home for the night. When the place had quieted down, Alex attacked the paperwork he'd been avoiding all week. That was hours ago, and he'd been working ever since.

He should at least stretch out on the couch and try to get some sleep. Last night and the long day were beginning to take their toll. He started to stand, and a slice of pain ripped through his right side. Sinking slowly back into his chair, he sucked in a short breath. He kept forgetting about the damned ribs.

Just then, he heard the center's outer door open and close.

Carefully this time, he stood and walked to his office door. It wasn't unusual for one of the neighborhood boys to come looking for a place to stay the night. He waited to see who it would be this time.

The last person he expected was Kristen.

She crossed the main room halfway and stopped, the dim night lights casting her in shadow. For several moments, neither of them spoke. Finally she said, "Are we alone?"

"Yes."

"I need to talk to you." Her voice possessed an edge he'd never heard before.

"Come in." He turned, walked back to his desk, and sat down, unsure how he felt about her showing up.

She followed, stepping into the office and the light for the first time. Tension lined her face. Something or someone had upset her. He thought immediately of Hector, and before he could stop himself, rose to go to her.

She raised a hand, palm out. "Don't. What I have to say won't take long."

Gripping the arms of his chair, he forced himself to sit back down. "What happened?"

She hesitated, her eyes wary as they searched his face. "Tell me about Seth Langford."

Alex settled back into his chair and sighed. Not Hector. She'd been talking to Frank Langford. "What do you want to know?"

Again the hesitation, briefer this time. "Did you kill him?"

He winced at the direct question, at the accusation in her voice. Though he couldn't blame her. For years he'd asked himself the same question. Finally, he'd been able to say truthfully, "No. I didn't kill him."

He saw the questions, the uncertainty ripple across her features. Then some of the tension left her. She believed him. As simply as that, he knew she believed him.

"Tell me about it." She sat on the edge of the couch across from his desk.

He thought for a moment. It had been so long ago, nearly eighteen years, but he remembered every detail. The cool, dark January night. The damp streets. The sound of footfalls—his and Seth's—racing along the sidewalk. The sirens and shouts. The shots. And Seth's scream as a bullet found its mark.

Even now Alex couldn't deny his part in that night's events. He'd been there, but Seth had made his own choices.

"There are no secrets here, Kristen," he said finally. "Nothing you couldn't learn from a dozen other sources. Frank Langford included."

"I want to hear it from you."

Alex took a deep breath. He would have given anything not to relive that night, but he couldn't refuse her. At least from him, she'd hear the truth. "You remember I told you

91

that I was caught breaking into a liquor store when I was eighteen?"

She nodded.

"Well, Seth was with me that night."

He saw the surprise on her face and shifted uncomfortably in his chair, ignoring the pain in his ribs, wishing it were as easy to ignore his memories. "Things were getting out of hand. *I* was getting out of hand. I was a petty thief and a con man."

"But you were a child."

"Was I? For years, I'd been putting food on my mother's table." He paused, and she started to say something, but he stopped her with a raised hand. "I know that sounds like an excuse, but it isn't. There were other things I could have done to help out. Stealing was easier. And . . ." He shrugged. "I liked it.

"But I was getting tired of the little stuff," he continued. "I decided to hit the liquor store." He laughed abruptly. "Not a particularly original idea. But it was a big step for me. It was a two-man job, and I'd always worked alone. So I put out the word on the street that I was looking for a partner. Seth volunteered." Alex shrugged. "He probably wanted to piss off Frank. They weren't on the best of terms at the time.

"Anyway, we triggered a silent alarm, and when the cops showed up, we ran. Seth died."

He waited for her reaction, for the realization of what he'd done to sink in and turn to revulsion. Instead, she said, "You didn't kill him."

She'd surprised him again, just as she'd done a dozen times or more since he'd met her. He doubted whether tales of kids robbing liquor stores and getting shot in the process was something she heard often—at least not in reference to someone she knew. He'd expected a negative response from her. Instead, he'd gotten understanding.

"Frankie blames me," he said. "The robbery was my idea, and Seth came with me to spite him." She started to object, but again, he cut her off. "But you're right, I didn't pull the trigger."

She sighed, closed her eyes, and leaned her head against the back of the couch. He could almost feel her confusion, her weariness. She'd come here expecting to tend to people's physical ills, not to become embroiled in his eighteen-year-old drama.

Standing, he crossed the room to sit next to her and take her hand. It was small and delicate with short, neatly trimmed nails. She had working hands.

He liked that about her. That and her boldness, her directness. And even her determination to help out in a neighborhood where half the population—himself included —didn't want her around.

"You talked to Langford," he said.

She nodded without opening her eyes. "He was waiting for me when I left the clinic this evening."

"I thought you were off today."

"I was. But I went down there, and they needed help." She shrugged. "Anyway, Detective Langford had some questions about missing drugs and equipment at the clinic."

"Are there drugs missing from the clinic?"

"I doubt it." Keeping her eyes closed, she shook her head. "At least, I don't think so. We do a daily count on all controlled substances. What he really wanted to ask me about was you."

"What about me?"

She opened her eyes then, searching his face, looking for

explanations he couldn't give her. "Nothing I could answer."

He held her gaze for several moments and wished things could be different. Another time and place perhaps. . . But he'd learned years before that wishing didn't change things. You had to play with whatever cards came up.

"What else did he say?"

She glanced away. "He just asked what I knew about you. I couldn't tell him much. Then I asked him what he had against you, and he said you'd killed his brother."

Alex fought down his anger. He understood Frankie's hatred of him and had tolerated it ever since coming home two years earlier. But why bring Kristen into their quarrel? She had nothing to do with it.

He realized she was still watching him. The trust in her eyes awed him, making him wonder what he'd done to deserve it. Ignoring the ache in his side, he reached over and traced the line of her cheek. Her skin was pale and clear, and as smooth as satin, yet warm. And soft. He'd never felt anything so soft.

"You look like you could use some sleep," he said, those deep green eyes of hers pulling at him.

"It's been a long week." Her words sounded forced, breathless.

He tried to think of all the reasons he shouldn't want this woman, why he should send her away before he did more than caress her cheek. It was no use. He wanted her with a fierceness he couldn't deny or ignore.

And he needed just one more taste.

He couldn't stop himself—or maybe he just didn't want to. Slowly, he lowered his head and brushed his mouth against hers, taking his time, wanting to savor her sweetness. As before, she responded, sighing as he skimmed her lips with his tongue, opening to him, inviting him to deepen the kiss.

Kristen's mind emptied when Alex touched her. She could no longer think. She could only feel—the gentle brush of his fingers against her skin, the sensuous flavor of his mouth. Kissing him was even more wonderful than she remembered, and she wanted it to go on forever. Reaching out, she rested her hand against his chest, feeling the hard strength beneath her fingertips, aching to explore, knowing if she started, neither of them would stop.

She drew back reluctantly.

Alex leaned his forehead against hers. "This is crazy."

She couldn't speak, couldn't find the breath to answer.

He pulled away, stood, and turned his back to her. But not before she saw just how much he wanted her.

"So much for our resolve to avoid each other," he said with a short, humorless laugh.

Again, she couldn't respond. Not with the desire still spiraling within her, urging her to go to him and wrap her arms around his waist, tempting her to forget everything but how much she wanted him.

"I don't imagine you're the kind of woman to have a casual affair." It wasn't a question. Not really.

She thought of her professor in medical school and how much more she wanted Alex. "No, I'm not."

"I didn't think so." He turned back to look at her and laughed abruptly again. "Although I don't suspect there would be anything casual about sex between us."

She smiled, feeling the heat tinge her cheeks.

"Come on." He offered her his hand. "I'll walk you out."

She took his hand, and the physical contrasts between them fascinated her. Large against small. Dark against light. Rough against smooth. A bit like their individual lives.

She pushed the thought aside and let him lead her out into the dimly lit main room, until they came to the computer tables. Stopping, she ran a hand over one of the brand-new laptops. "I assume these aren't just so the kids can play computer games."

He laughed briefly. "I expect there will be some of that, but we'll keep a lid on it."

"Good luck with that."

"Seriously though, the kids in this neighborhood are at a disadvantage to those from more affluent areas. Our schools are underequipped and understaffed. The best way to help these boys is to give them the tools and the training to compete. That's what we're trying to do with this equipment."

"And the training?"

"I have a contact at the local community college, and he's found us a few volunteers to come in and give classes. We'll start with basic applications, but I'd also like to see some of these kids learn about graphics or even programming. And this equipment . . . it's just the beginning."

It was an ambitious plan, but for some reason, Kristen knew he'd pull it off . . . if he had the funding.

They started toward the door again, and after a few steps, Kristen said, "Alex, where do you get the money to run the center and buy equipment?"

He frowned, but before he could say anything, she quickly added, "I'm not trying to pry. I just have some ideas of how you can get more backing."

He hesitated, obviously uncomfortable talking about the center's finances. Finally, he said, "LJ and I bought the building using our early retirement pay. Since then, we've been pretty much dependent on private donations from individuals and organizations."

They arrived at her car, and he released her hand, slipping his own into the pockets of his jeans. "We've also solicited funds from federal and state agencies, but without much success. The few times they've approved us, the money came with more strings than a third-rate puppet show." He pulled a hand from his pockets and ran it through his hair. "See, I don't have the contacts or the credentials to warrant funding. I'm from the neighborhood, so how could I possibly know what these kids need? Now, if I were an outsider, or a Ph.D. who'd spent half my life in a classroom . . ."

He didn't finish, but he didn't have to. Kristen understood all too well how the system worked. Her father was a master at manipulating it, and watching him, she'd learned a thing or two over the years. "What if I can help with the private donations?"

Alex sighed. "We've been over this before, Kristen. I don't want your money."

"That's not what I meant. I know people who—"

"Forget it. You're doing enough around here already between working at the clinic and visiting shut-ins. LJ and I are managing the center just fine." Taking her keys from her, he unlocked and opened her car door. "Come on." He nodded for her to get in. "It's getting late."

* * *

Kristen rolled over and looked at her bedside clock. Half past three. She'd been tossing and turning since one-thirty. In another couple of hours, she'd have to get up again in order to be back at the clinic by six. But, once again, sleep had eluded her as her thoughts spun around Alex Jamison.

Every time she closed her eyes, she saw him: the darkness of his eyes and hair, the broadness of his chest and shoulders. With a little concentration she could almost hear the deep timbre of his voice, feel his rough hands against her cheek, and taste the keen hunger of his mouth.

She couldn't make herself believe that kissing him again had been a mistake. It had felt too good, too right. For the first time, she understood all the fuss about sexual attraction. One look from Alex and her insides turned to mush; one touch, and she lost all sense of reality.

Still, there was more to this attraction than the physical.

Lust, she could ignore. The other things she felt for Alex weren't as easily put aside. Things like respect and friendship.

It would seem that the more she learned about him, the more she'd realize how unsuited they were for each other. Instead, with each new discovery, she found herself drawn more strongly to him. She knew her peers would tell her it didn't make sense, but Kristen thought she understood.

Caring, giving of yourself, came easily when you'd had loving parents and all the advantages money could buy. Alex had had neither. Yet, he cared. Maybe too much. Enough to turn his life around and dedicate it to kids who needed help. How could she help but love him?

No! Not love. How could she love a man she'd known less than a week? Respect and friendship was what she felt for Alex. That, mixed with the wild sexual chemistry between them, was dangerous enough.

As for her idea of how to help him with his youth center, she couldn't let that go either. The thought had taken hold of her, resisting any attempt to dislodge it.

Her father's birthday gala was in three weeks, with hundreds of wealthy guests invited. She couldn't ask for donations at the party, but she could introduce Alex around. She knew several women who spent their lives putting together fund-raising events. If she could get one of them interested in his youth center, his kids would get all the computers they could use. Along with any other equipment they needed.

The problem wasn't going to be getting things rolling in Palm Beach, it would be getting Alex to go along with the idea. He'd have to agree to come with her to the party, and considering his reaction every time she mentioned helping out, convincing him wasn't going to be easy.

Finally, she gave up trying to sleep.

Throwing off the covers, she pulled on a robe and headed downstairs. She'd go into the clinic early.

There was always paperwork that needed doing. But first, she needed food and lots of hot coffee. Those two things had kept her going through medical school. They'd just have to get her past Alex Jamison as well.

* * *

Alex waited in the hot August sun, watching the dark clouds build on the western horizon. This time of year, late afternoon thunderstorms occurred daily. They rolled in off the Everglades in a rush of torrential wind and rain, leaving behind a heat that simmered from the wet pavement.

Today it was moving in early.

Alex had managed to stay away from Langford for a full twelve hours after sending Kristen home last night. Twelve hours of no sleep and an anger building inside him like the ominous clouds of the storm. He wanted a few words with Detective Frank Langford, and he needed to have them in a place with a lot of witnesses.

For both their sakes.

So Alex had done some checking and learned that Langford ate at the same storefront diner on Miami Beach every day. It was just a matter of getting over there at lunchtime and waiting for him to appear.

At twelve-thirty, Alex took up his post in a parking lot on Collins Avenue, next to Langford's city-issued car. About fifteen minutes later, Langford came strolling out of the restaurant across the street, dressed in an immaculate summer-weight suit. He stopped when he spotted Alex, his hatred palpable even at a hundred yards. A moment later, he started walking again, crossing the street to where Alex waited.

"What are you doing here, Jamison?"

Alex folded his arms across his chest and leaned back against the other man's car. "Looking for you."

"Should I be flattered?"

"Hardly."

A low roll of thunder rumbled in the distance, and Alex glanced at the sky. "Looks like we're in for a good one this afternoon."

"What do you want?"

Alex turned back to the other man. "I thought it was time we had a little chat."

"I don't have anything to say to you."

"But I have something to say to you. Stay away from Kristen Helton."

"You mean, *Dr.* Helton?"

"You know exactly who I mean."

"And why would I want to do that?" With his hands in his pockets, Langford rocked back and forth on his heels. "She's an attractive woman. Great body. All that fiery red hair. Makes a man wonder." He paused, evidently to let his implications sink in while considering Kristen Helton's assets himself. "Oh, and she's rich too."

Alex refused to take the bait. Langford would like nothing better than to arrest him for assaulting a police officer—which was exactly what would happen if Alex took a swing at the other man. Instead, he said, "She's got no role in your little melodrama."

"I'm not so sure about that. Besides, what's it to you?" Langford laughed scornfully. "You don't think she'd be interested in a loser like you. Do you?"

"What's between Kristen and me is none of your business." Alex pushed away from the car and pulled himself to his full height. "Just stay away from her."

"Tell me, Jamison. What are you into these days? Dealing? Fencing?" Langford paused, his grin failing to hide the menace behind his words. "Or are you still robbing liquor stores?"

Thunder, closer now, rumbled around them, while a streak of lightning split the western sky.

Alex took a step forward. "You want a piece of me, Frankie? Go ahead and take the first shot."

"Looks to me like someone already took you up on that. Did a little damage to your eye." Langford crossed his arms. "Makes me wonder just what kind of people you're dealing with."

Alex went cold inside. "Keep out of my way, Frankie. And stay away from Kristen Helton."

"Is that a threat?"

"No. A promise." With that, he spun on his heel, oblivious to the sudden onslaught of rain as he put distance between himself and Frank Langford. Otherwise, Alex might just change his mind about keeping his hands to himself.

Chapter Eight

It had been two weeks since Kristen had seen Alex, fourteen long days since he'd told her about Seth Langford.

From her penthouse terrace, she watched the late afternoon storm move in from the west. Dark, bilious clouds pushed their way toward the Atlantic, blocking the sun and turning a crystalline blue sky dingy and gray. Thunder rumbled, and a flash of distant lightning briefly brightened the Miami skyline. A few minutes more, Kristen thought, and she'd go in.

At the moment, however, the approaching storm fit her mood.

She knew Alex was purposely avoiding her, carrying through with what they'd agreed was the best thing for both of them: staying away from each other. That didn't mean she liked it.

Somewhere along the line, she'd lost her resolve to keep her distance from him. She could still list all the reasons they shouldn't pursue a relationship, but she no longer cared. She wanted Alex and had decided to take a chance.

Meanwhile, he'd chosen now to disappear, to step out of her life.

At the same time, he'd kept his promise to set up meetings with other housebound patients, sending LJ or one of the older boys with information about anyone who needed a doctor. And on the days she visited Elena, she'd find LJ waiting for her beneath the huge banyan tree across the street. With his quick smile and easy manner, he'd walk her the few blocks, keeping her laughing the whole way.

But he wasn't Alex.

At the end of the first week, she'd considered confronting him. His location was no secret. If she really wanted to see him, she could make the short walk from the clinic to the youth center. He couldn't very well ignore her if she showed up on his doorstep.

Somehow, she'd managed to talk herself out of it, telling herself he was doing the right thing. Eventually, the chemistry between them would fade. It had to.

By the end of the second week, however, she hadn't been so sure. The need to see him had become a constant ache. At odd moments she'd find herself idly staring out one of the clinic's windows, wondering what he was doing. Or as she walked to the parking lot in the evening, she'd look over at the youth center, listening for the sounds of male voices coming from the basketball court. Each night she'd tell herself she wouldn't stop today—maybe tomorrow—and she'd climb into her car and head home. Granted, there was some pride involved. If he could avoid her for this long, then she could be just as strong.

Now it was Sunday, the beginning of the third week, and her will to stay away from him had vanished.

Another crash of thunder, followed by a bright flash of lightning, brought her out of her thoughts. Overhead, the dark clouds had won their claim on the day and, at any moment, would open up and drench the earth.

Kristen headed for the covered portion of the patio, just making it before a veil of water fell from the sky. She stood for several minutes, her arms wrapped around her waist against the sudden chill, and watched the rain.

She'd wait one more day, until she left the clinic tomorrow night. If he didn't come to see her by then, she'd go to him.

* * *

Monday dawned overcast and muggy.

At the clinic, the patients were few and far between, evidently finding it too much trouble to venture out in the damp heat even for medical care. Kristen, too, felt the weight of the inclement weather. Her determination to seek out Alex hung over her like the gray clouds over the city.

She knew she should be relieved to have finally made the decision to confront him. Unfortunately, underneath her resolve was fear. If he told her he wanted nothing more to do with her, she'd have to accept it, and just the thought frightened her more than she liked to admit. That was a whole six or eight hours away, however, and she wouldn't let herself spend the day expecting the worst. She'd always been an optimist, and now wasn't the time to change.

Besides, she had her trip to see Elena to look forward to. Her Spanish lessons three times a week had become one of the highlights of Kristen's days at the clinic.

Then she got a text from LJ. He couldn't get away to walk her to Elena's at the usual time but would be down in the afternoon. She considered waiting, but finally decided against it. She'd visited Elena at the same time for three full weeks now without any sign of trouble. She hadn't even seen Hector since that first day. It seemed ridiculous to depend on LJ or anyone else to escort her. Sooner or later, she needed to start relying on herself. Besides, Elena was expecting her that morning, not in the afternoon, and Kristen badly needed to get out for a while.

A couple of hours later, Kristen was happy she hadn't waited. She'd cleaned and redressed Elena's almost healed arm, and they'd had a particularly interesting Spanish lesson.

"You are a good girl," Elena said as Kristen got ready to leave. "You learn quickly."

Kristen smiled. "I have a good teacher."

"Soon you will speak like you were born in Cuba."

Kristen laughed. "I don't know about that . . ."

"Well, maybe not that good." Elena grinned. "But you will manage. And this . . ." She held up her hand and broke into a huge smile. *"Gracias."*

"It wasn't a serious burn, Elena. It would have—"

"Not the burn." She flexed her hand. "It has been a long time since I could do that, *Doctora."*

Pleasure heated Kristen's cheeks. It was one of the nicest compliments anyone had ever paid her. In all the time she'd been coming to see Elena, the older woman had never addressed her as doctor.

"Elena," she started to say, unsure of how to put her thought, "I—"

"Hector!" Elena interrupted.

Kristen's heart seemed to momentarily stop, then began to beat furiously as she followed Elena's gaze.

Hector stood in the doorway.

"Por favor, Hector," Elena said. "Come, sit with your old *abuelita."*

* * *

Alex parked in front of the center and glanced across the street at the clinic's parking lot. Kristen's little white rental sat in its usual place. Climbing out of the van, he looked toward the clinic, thinking he might catch sight of her— even though he knew it was too late: a half hour too late. LJ would have already walked with her over to Elena's house. And that's the way Alex wanted it, the way he'd planned it.

Damn!

What the hell was he doing hoping to catch glimpses of her every chance he got? He laughed abruptly and without humor at the stupid question.

Two weeks ago, he'd convinced himself that avoiding her would eventually get easier. Yet each time he'd sent LJ to escort her around the neighborhood, it got harder not to go himself. Each time he'd fought the little voice whispering inside his head that it wouldn't hurt just to see her—in the middle of the day—for the short walk between the clinic and Elena's house.

He knew better.

Seeing her would make him want her again. Like an addict, one little taste of being around her wouldn't be enough. He'd want more. In theory, the longer he stayed away from her, the sooner he'd forget her heart-stopping smile, the way her green eyes flashed, the sweet taste of her kiss. It was a great idea. In theory. Except it wasn't working.

With each passing day the need to see her grew stronger, not weaker. Today, he'd forced himself to stay away from the center until late morning, knowing LJ would have already left to pick her up at the clinic. The temptation had just become too strong to be around when LJ headed out. Once again, Alex had accomplished his goal, while wishing he'd failed.

Inside the center, it surprised him to find LJ lodged beneath a sink in the small kitchen area. "What's going on?" Alex asked. "How come you're still here?"

"Busted pipe. There was water all over when I got in this morning. Thought I might have to start issuing life jackets."

Alex crouched down beside his friend. "You should have called me."

LJ grunted but didn't reply.

"What about Kristen?"

"I sent a text telling her to wait until this afternoon."

"Did she agree?"

"No, but . . ." LJ shifted his head out from under the pipes, looking at Alex for the first time. "Why? Is there a problem?"

Alex stood and ran a hand through his hair. He couldn't blame LJ. Alex had put the responsibility for Kristen's safety on his friend too long. "Only that she probably didn't wait. If I know Kristen, she went on her own."

"She's a big girl." LJ wiped his hands on a rag and scooted out from under the sink. "And I've walked her over there a half dozen times in the last couple of weeks. There's been no trouble, and no sign of Hector."

"Just because things have been quiet is no reason to believe they'll stay that way. Hector's not about to suddenly welcome her with open arms."

LJ turned on the faucet and crouched down to look beneath the sink. "Damn, I'm good. Dry as a bone."

Alex shook his head. "Modesty was never one of your faults."

"Nor yours, my friend." LJ stood and shut off the water.

"As for Hector, aren't you the one who's always telling me he's an okay kid underneath that smart mouth and volatile temper?"

Alex fought a sardonic grin. "I'd hate to risk Kristen's safety on my evaluation of Hector's finer points."

"I think you're worried about nothing." LJ shrugged. "But if you're so concerned, you should start taking her yourself. Besides, it might do wonders for the lousy mood you've been in for the past two weeks."

Alex couldn't deny it. He'd been a real jerk lately, grumbling at the least provocation. The more timid boys had steered clear of him, while others seemed to delight in rattling his cage, just to see what it took to snap his temper. He knew what the problem was, and obviously so did LJ.

Kristen.

Or, more precisely, the fact that he hadn't seen her in two weeks. Turning, he headed for the door.

"Where are you going?" LJ called.

"I'm going to make sure the good doctor doesn't get herself into any more trouble."

* * *

"Come, Hector," Elena said again. "Join us."

Kristen swore she saw something soft in Hector's eyes, a genuine warmth as he looked at his grandmother. Then he shifted his gaze to Kristen, and his features turned hard and unyielding. It was as if he'd forgotten for a moment to be angry and needed to correct the situation.

"Not now, Grandmother. I got things to do." He spun on his heel and started for the front door.

Kristen stood, not understanding her sudden urge to go after him, but wanting to nonetheless. "Elena, do you mind?" she asked, glancing at the older woman. "I'd like to talk to Hector for a minute."

"Go, go," Elena said, shooing her away. "I see you in a couple of days."

Kristen caught up with him in the front yard. "Hector, wait!"

He surprised her by stopping, but when he turned around to face her, she wished she'd let him go. Anger and suspicion shadowed his face. "What do you want, *gringa?*"

Holding out her hands palms up, she said, "I just want to talk."

He laughed abruptly, bitterly. "What would we possibly have to say to each other?"

"It's about your grandmother."

"My grandmother? That crazy old lady. Maybe you want me to gush all over you like she did? Tell you what a good job you've done, helping with her arthritis?" He took a menacing step toward her. "Do you get off on that, *gringa?* Having us lowlifes grovel at your feet?"

Kristen held her ground, though she couldn't for the life of her figure out why. The smartest thing to do would be to apologize and head back to the clinic. She did neither of those things. Instead, she said, "All I wanted to say was that I appreciate your letting me visit your grandmother."

He scowled. "What choice did I have? The old woman is *loco.* She burned herself because she wouldn't go see no doctor for her arthritis."

"You had a choice. I know you didn't want me here. You could have made it impossible for me to spend time with her. But you didn't."

With a sweep of his hand he brushed her words aside. "Look, why you bothering me?"

Kristen ignored the question. "She told me you took her

109

to church yesterday. She said it was the first time she'd been out of the house in nearly a year."

Hesitation flickered across his features, and then denial took its place. "I didn't go to no church."

"But you *took* your grandmother."

"So?"

"So, it was good of you."

Again, he hesitated, his eyes narrowing as if trying to figure her out. "You know what I think, *gringa?*" He moved in closer, so close she could feel the heat radiating from his skin. For some reason, she wasn't afraid and momentarily questioned her own sanity. "I think you're as crazy as that old woman. Maybe crazier."

"What's going on here?"

Kristen jumped, then swung around as Alex closed the distance between them.

Hector cursed. "I'm out of here, man."

"No, wait—" Kristen started to call after him, but it was too late. He'd disappeared behind the house. She spun on Alex, who stood glaring after the boy. "What the hell did you do that for?"

"Do what?" Alex crossed his arms and turned his intimidating stare on her. "Keep that crazy kid from assaulting you again?"

"He was not assaulting me."

"Not yet."

Kristen barely controlled her anger. She'd made a small crack in Hector's armor, getting him to actually stand for a few minutes and talk with her—even if he wasn't hearing what she had to say. Then Alex had come barreling in, looking to save the day. Who knew when—or if—she'd get another opportunity to win Hector over.

"You know," she said, "if you weren't so hell-bent on

throwing your weight around, you might have noticed what was really going on here." She turned away from him, starting across the yard and heading back to the clinic.

Alex followed. "Oh, yeah? And what was that?"

"We were talking."

He laughed abruptly. "You and Hector? Right. I'm sure you've become best friends."

She didn't dignify his comment with a reply. Especially since she doubted whether she could speak civilly right now anyway.

After a moment Alex said, "What were you doing there by yourself anyway? If you'd waited—"

"Please, Alex." She lifted a hand to cut him off. "I know you mean well, but I don't need a babysitter."

He laughed abruptly.

She stopped short and turned on him. "Look, I appreciate all you've done, but things have been going very well lately. People are starting to get used to me in the neighborhood, and at this point I'm perfectly capable of taking care of myself."

"It didn't look that way a moment ago."

"As I said, we were just—"

"Yeah, yeah I know. Talking."

Kristen closed her eyes and counted to ten. When she opened them again, Alex was still there. For two weeks, she'd been agonizing over this man's absence. She must have lost her mind. He was infuriating, and right now she wished he'd just go away.

Alex watched her attempt to control her temper. God, she was something else when she was angry. He figured that would be his downfall where she was concerned. Those eyes of hers, and the way they seemed to spit emerald fire.

He could see himself purposely setting her off, just to witness the fireworks.

"Look," he said, realizing she had a point about Hector —maybe he had rushed in too quickly. He'd just gone a little nuts when he'd seen Hector snapping at her like an angry pit bull. "I'm sorry. Okay? I was just worried about you."

He watched the heat drain from her anger. "I know." She shook her head and said, "But what is it with you two? I mean, it took me a while, but I'm beginning to understand why Hector's wary of me. I'm an outsider, and he can't quite figure out what I'm doing here. What I want."

She paused, pressing her lips together while her gaze wandered past him for a moment. When she looked back at him, she added, "But what about you? Why does he hate you?"

Alex took a deep breath. She wanted information half the neighborhood took for granted, but he felt like he was baring his soul. "I made a mistake with Hector when I first came back to the neighborhood. One I'm still paying for."

She nodded. "Go on."

"I knew immediately he was a strong kid, a leader. And I set out to befriend him."

"But it didn't work."

He slipped his hands into the back pockets of his jeans. "It worked. Until the night I caught him with a Rolex on his wrist."

"A Rolex?"

"A gold one." He figured she knew the particular style he meant. "At the time, it was worth about ten grand in any upscale jewelry store. Maybe half that on the street."

"Where did he get it?"

Alex shrugged. "Well, now, that's the question, isn't it? He said he was wearing it for a few hours, just until he could get rid of it. He wanted to know how the gold felt. He was thirteen."

"What did you do?"

"I figured there was only one way he could have gotten his hands on that watch. So I did what any self-righteous idiot would do. I turned him in."

Her eyes widened.

"Yeah, I know, it was stupid. But I thought it would straighten him out. Hell, it worked for me." He looked down at the sidewalk. "So much for playing amateur psychologist."

She turned and started walking again, slower this time, as if she'd lost her energy as well as her anger. Alex knew how she felt.

After a few minutes of awkward silence he said, "So, how have you been?"

She hesitated briefly, almost unnoticeably. "Great. And you?"

"Oh, me too. Just great." They walked a bit farther, each occupied with their own thoughts.

Finally, Alex mumbled a curse. "Actually, that's a lie. It's been a hell of a two weeks." He caught her quick sideways glance and smiled sheepishly. "I've been in a lousy mood. Not even LJ wants anything to do with me."

She laughed shortly. "Is that something new?"

He grinned. "Yeah. Since you showed up in the neighborhood."

She flushed and looked away. "I've got a confession to make as well."

"You've been in a lousy mood too?" he teased.

"No." She laughed. "I'm not particularly moody like some people we know. But . . ."

"But?" He stopped and caught her hand.

"I had planned on coming over to the youth center tonight." She suddenly seemed uncharacteristically shy, and it tugged at his heart.

"And?" he prodded.

She shook her head, obviously embarrassed. "I was planning on demanding that you either stop avoiding me, or tell me in person to get lost."

He laughed, picturing the way her eyes would have flashed when she issued her ultimatum. He was almost sorry he'd missed it. He draped an arm around her shoulders, and they started walking again. "That's not what would have happened, you know."

"Really?"

"I probably would have dragged you down on that ratty old vinyl couch and ravished you."

"Ravished me?" She grinned up at him. "Oh, dear."

He had a hard time restraining himself from doing that just then. He would have at least liked a quick taste of those delectable lips of hers.

Instead, he kept walking.

"So what are we going to do about this?" he asked. "About us?"

She shot him another sideways glance. "Is there an 'us'?"

"Isn't there?" He sighed and slipped his free hand into his front jeans pocket. "I keep listing all the reasons I should keep my hands off you, but . . ." He shrugged. "It's a losing battle."

"Maybe we should stop fighting it."

He stopped again and turned her to look at him. "You think that's a good idea?"

"Probably not, but why don't we just see what happens?"

"You *know* what will happen."

"Would that be so terrible?" She smiled. "Besides . . ." She started walking. "Don't be so sure of yourself. I'm not that easy."

He laughed, feeling lighter than he had in weeks, and caught up to her. "Okay, so how about dinner tonight?"

They'd reached the clinic, and she stopped again. "On one condition."

"Name it."

"Come with me to Palm Beach this weekend. My mother is throwing a party for my father for his sixtieth birthday."

"I don't know . . ." Alex shook his head. "I don't think I'm quite ready for the 'meet the parents' thing."

"Not to meet my parents. It'll give us time with lots of people around, and—" She hesitated. "And you can meet some people who can help you financially with the center."

He couldn't believe she wouldn't let this go. "Kristen—"

"No, wait," she cut him off. "I've been thinking about this since the night you showed me the laptops."

Again, he started to object.

"Please." She touched his arm. "Just hear me out."

He nodded reluctantly. What else could he do when she looked at him like that? "Okay, go ahead."

"Every year, my mother throws a huge party for my father's birthday. It's become a major social event in Palm Beach. Some of the wealthiest people in the state will be there."

"That's exactly why it's not a good idea for me to come with you."

"That's *exactly* why you should go. These people donate millions of dollars a year to charitable organizations. Why not to your youth center?"

Before he could comment, she rushed on. "You told me yourself that the center depends on private donations. I can introduce you to people with more money than they know what to do with. We can tell them about the youth center and the good work you're doing. You can't pass this up, Alex."

She was right—though he'd like to turn her down anyway. He didn't like mixing money, the center, and Kristen all together. He would have liked to keep them separate. But then, nothing had gone the way he'd expected since Kristen had first walked into his life.

"Okay," he said. "I'll go."

She broke into a huge smile, and it was almost worth it just to see that smile.

"But I have my own condition," he added. "What's that?"

"That," he said, bending down to give her a quick kiss good-bye, "is my secret."

Chapter Nine

The elevator stopped, and the doors slid silently open.

Alex stepped out into a pristine, marble-floored outer foyer. It was a bit overwhelming, like glacial ice, softened only by large vases of fresh flowers set on wall insets on either side of massive double doors.

Just as he went to knock, a uniformed woman opened the door.

"Good evening, Mr. Jamison," she said, moving aside so he could enter.

It unnerved him, being greeted at the door by a house-keeper who knew his name and anticipated his arrival. Hell, just the idea of servants of any kind disturbed him, but he kept his discomfort to himself and stepped into a gracious two-story inner foyer.

Again, the entire room seemed made of white marble: floors, walls, the sweeping curved staircase, even a table set beneath a crystal chandelier with another huge vase of fresh flowers. It was more than he'd expected in a condominium. No matter the location or price tag.

"Is Dr. Helton ready?" he asked, trying to sound unaffected by the wealthy surroundings.

"She'll be down in a minute, sir. Can I get you anything while you wait?"

"No, thank you."

She motioned toward a room off to the left. "Please have a seat in the living room, and I'll tell Dr. Helton that you've arrived."

The woman moved off, leaving Alex to find his own way into the next room.

He thought he'd prepared himself for the inside of the Helton apartment. After all, he'd been to the homes of wealthy people before, to receptions and dinners where he'd solicited funds for the center. Nothing, however, could have prepared him for the inside of Kristen's home. Not *her* home, he reminded himself, her parents'. Though knowing it didn't belong to her did nothing to alleviate his discomfort. Maybe it was just the fact that Kristen lived there, and the woman he'd come to know seemed as far removed from this place as he himself.

Yet, he knew that wasn't true.

This was where she belonged. In this beautifully appointed apartment, with its white-on-white decor and twenty-foot floor-to-ceiling windows overlooking a patio with the Atlantic Ocean as a backdrop.

He had to ask himself once again, what the hell was he doing here? What was he doing with this woman? Thinking about her? Wanting her? The last week with her had been like living a dream, a fantasy of the type Alex never allowed himself. He no more belonged with her than—

"Alex?"

He turned at the sound of her voice, and the sight of her hit him like a punch.

She was a temptress in green silk that wrapped around her neck with tiny straps, then dipped dangerously low across her breasts before dropping dramatically to her high-heeled feet, clinging to every curve along the way. She moved toward him, revealing one long, sexy leg through a slit that cut to her thigh.

Thinking was no longer an option. As long as he was around her, no amount of rational thought could change the way he wanted her.

A light blush touched her cheek, and she said, "You're staring."

"You're beautiful."

She laughed softly and closed the distance between them. "I guess that's an acceptable excuse."

He reached up and claimed a silky tendril of hair that had escaped the mass of curls she'd piled atop her head. Then he let his fingers wander to caress the ivory skin of her neck. He heard her breath catch and took pleasure in seeing the clear green of her eyes cloud with desire.

"We could stay here," she said, and her voice, usually so practical and straightforward, held wisps of seduction and eagerness all wrapped together.

"Could we?" He moved to trace her mouth with his thumb, parting her lips as her eyes fluttered shut. "But then I wouldn't have the chance to show you off."

"Does that matter?"

"Not to me." He brushed her lips lightly with his. He had no choice; they drew him like a parched man to water. "But it's important to you."

"Alex—"

He stopped her words with another kiss—sweet, so sweet—and whispered against her mouth, "You promised your parents we would be there."

"I'll tell them something came up."

He groaned, tempted. "It would be the truth."

"Alex . . ." It came out as another whisper.

He claimed another kiss, cradling her face with his hands, drinking from her lips, tasting her tongue. He held on, knowing if he let go, if he let his hands wander, move over her body like they wanted, he wouldn't stop. *They* wouldn't stop. They'd end up making love right there on the floor, in a puddle of green silk.

Finally, he found the strength to release her mouth, and she sighed, letting her head tilt forward to rest her forehead against his shoulder.

"We should go," he said, though he didn't sound convinced.

"Yes," she agreed.

Somehow, he managed to step away, the ache in his groin a reminder of what he was giving up.

She looked up at him, her green eyes clearing. "Sooner or later . . ."

She didn't need to say anything more. He understood. They were headed toward the inevitable, toward satisfying this hunger they both felt. Maybe, as she'd suggested, he should stop fighting it. Maybe the best way to purge it from their systems was to let it happen. Only, next to his need sat fear, fear that once he'd made love to her, once he'd eased himself inside her, he'd never want to release her.

He stepped back and offered her his arm in a gesture as stiff and formal as the tradition itself. "Shall we go?"

They rode the elevator in silence down to the first floor, where the doorman escorted them outside. A sleek black limousine sat in front, and the driver jumped out and circled around to them.

Kristen looked at Alex, a question in her eyes.

He smiled and motioned toward the door as the driver opened it. "Kristen?"

She moved forward, and he took her elbow to help her. Then he climbed in behind her, and the driver shut the door.

The champagne he'd ordered sat waiting in an ice bucket.

"How—" she started to say, but he stopped her, touching her lips briefly with two fingers.

"No questions," he said. He pulled the chilled bottle of Perrier-Jouet from the ice. "This is my condition for going with you. Tonight, we live the fantasy."

Live the fantasy.

Kristen sank back against the plush leather seats, the words echoing in her head as the car started moving. Alex poured the champagne, handing her the first glass.

She sipped the wine, knowing the price tag had been exorbitant, well beyond what Alex could afford. But she kept her thoughts to herself, watching him as he poured himself a glass and settled back beside her.

He looked wonderful, dark and mysteriously sexy. She'd always liked tuxedos; they seemed to give even the most unimpressive of men a certain amount of presence. On someone like Alex, the effect was devastating. He looked as if he'd been born to wear one.

He wanted her to accept this night without question, to live a fantasy with him. The limousine. The driver. The champagne. He offered them to her as if he were a man who could always give her these things. To live the fantasy, as he'd said. But limos and drivers and hundred-dollar bottles of champagne weren't fantasy to her. They existed in her everyday life. Or could, if that's what she chose, but she hadn't chosen them. She didn't want these things, or the kind of man who usually came with them.

She wanted Alex.

It suddenly seemed so clear. She'd fallen in love with him. When and where it had happened, she couldn't say. Somewhere between the time he'd first stepped between her and Hector Gonzales and the moment she'd entered the living room of her parents' penthouse apartment and seen Alex standing there in a black tuxedo. She wanted him. Not just physically—though that need ached through her on a constant basis—but all of him. More than she had any right to want or ask.

She sipped her wine, a deep sadness creeping over her. She should be happy. After all, she didn't fall in love every day. In fact, this was a first.

Alex reached over and claimed her free hand. "Do you want to talk about it?"

She turned to look at him, and he smiled softly, almost sadly. As if he could read her thoughts.

She shook her head. "No." They'd do it his way. "Tonight we live the fantasy." She smiled, imagining that there could be some kind of future, some happiness for the two of them.

* * *

Thirty minutes later, they turned into the long driveway of a Palm Beach mansion. In front of them, a half dozen other sleek vehicles waited to pull up to the house and drop off their passengers. As the slow parade inched forward, Alex's tension mounted. Kristen had grown up in a world as foreign to him as if she'd come from another planet, and in another few minutes, that fact would be in his face.

Then he remembered why he'd agreed to come: the contacts he'd make for the center. Though there was more to it than that. He'd come for Kristen too.

Finally, their limo stopped at the front of the house and the driver opened the door for them.

Alex felt like a fraud. He didn't belong here. This was a charade, and a smart man would cut his losses and take off. Instead, he turned, reached back into the automobile, and offered Kristen his hand. She exited the car, despite her full-length gown, with all the grace and ease of long practice. She belonged here.

Then she slipped her arm through his and smiled.

It was as if she could read his mind. She'd walked this same road, surviving on his turf for weeks. Now she'd asked him to do the same.

They walked up the steps to the mansion entrance. "Rough childhood," he said under his breath, trying to make light of the situation.

She laughed and squeezed his arm.

They'd reached the entry, where a butler stood greeting guests. "Miss Helton," he said. "It's so good to see you. Your mother has been asking for you."

"Thank you, Frederick." Nodding toward Alex, she added, "May I introduce Alejandro Jamison. Alex, Frederick has been with the family for years."

"Good to meet you, sir."

Alex hadn't the faintest idea how to respond, having never been introduced to a family servant before. He knew such people existed—in the movies, books—but this was real, all too real for comfort. He nodded and said, "Good evening, Frederick."

It must have been enough, because the man smiled, and Kristen moved them into the press of well-dressed people.

He'd thought the condo impressive. Compared to this, it was exactly as Kristen had described it: a weekend getaway. He knew if he let himself think about it—this house and the money behind it—he'd call off the whole thing right now. He'd turn on his heel and head on back to Miami. Where he belonged.

So he didn't think about it. Or look around too closely.

Instead, as he and Kristen circulated, he got the impression of sweeping rooms, high ceilings, and marble. Like the condominium, it was the flooring of choice, in cool white and subtle gray. Other than that, the rooms were awash in color. Women in gowns: long, short, sleek, or flowing. Men in tuxedos. And the jewelry. If he'd been a thief intent on making his fortune in one night, this party would have been a sure thing.

His practiced eye noticed the bulldogs scattered amid the crowd: big men looking uncomfortable in their formal clothing but at ease with their earplugs. They tried to remain inconspicuous, hovering on the fringes of the crowd, but anyone who bothered to look would notice them. Alex, evidently, was the only one looking.

"Well, well, Kristen, what do we have here?"

Stopping, she turned toward a man lounging against a wall near a large potted palm.

"Gregory!" Releasing Alex's arm, she stepped forward and kissed the other man on the cheek. "How are you?"

"The same." He returned the peck and, looking at Alex, said, "You, however, seem to be doing much better. Aren't you going to introduce us?"

"If I must." She laughed lightly and slipped her arm through his. "Alex, this is my cousin. Gregory Helton. Gregory, Alex Jamison."

"I think we've met," Gregory said, looking closely at Alex. "Haven't we?"

Alex forced a smile and extended his hand, even as a tendril of unease coiled in his gut. "I don't think so."

"From a distance, perhaps?"

"I'm afraid not," Alex answered, his unease growing. Why hadn't he seen this coming? He hadn't even considered the possibility that someone here would recognize him —and he should have.

"Alex doesn't spend much time this far north," Kristen said, moving back to his side. "He runs a youth center in Miami."

"Hmm. Well, I've been wrong before," Gregory said, though his eyes told another story. He knew Alex. Who he was. What he was. "And you." Gregory turned back to Kristen. "I hear you've been giving your father fits."

"No more than usual."

"Working in a free clinic down in Miami. How wonderfully clever of you, Kristen. I never thought you had it in you."

"Please, Gregory."

"You see"—he turned back to Alex—"I was the black sheep of the family. That is, until little Miss Florence Nightingale here decided to go to medical school. I don't think I'll ever forgive her for that." He hesitated before taking one more stab at Alex. "Are you sure we've never met?"

"Positive."

"Oh, there's Mother," Kristen said, nodding toward the far side of the room. "We really should go say hello, Gregory. We'll talk later."

"Be sure of it."

Kristen drew Alex farther into the crowd. "Don't let Gregory bother you," she said. "He's harmless."

Alex doubted it.

They made their way toward a tall, graceful woman standing among several couples. The group dispersed as Alex and Kristen got closer, and Alex noticed the green eyes and red hair—an older version of Kristen.

Mother and daughter hugged briefly, and Kristen said, "You look wonderful, Mother."

Carolyn Helton laughed lightly, looking more like Kristen's older sister than her mother. "You too. Though in my case it's amazing what makeup and the correct lighting can do."

"No need to fish for compliments, Mother. You're as beautiful as ever, and you know it."

She grinned. "Sounds like a compliment to me."

Kristen laughed and shifted back to Alex's side. "Mother, I want you to meet Alejandro Jamison. Alex, this is my mother, Carolyn Helton."

Carolyn extended her hand and smiled—her daughter's smile. "It's good to meet you, Mr. Jamison."

"Mrs. Helton." He took her hand and returned her smile.

"Please," she said, laughing. "Mrs. Helton is my mother-in-law. Call me Carolyn."

She'd charmed him, as simply as that, as easily as her daughter. "Then you can call me Alex."

She moved alongside him and took his arm. "I'm afraid my daughter has been somewhat remiss in telling us anything about you, Alex."

"Mother." There was a warning in Kristen's voice.

"Oh, don't worry, Kristen darling, I'm not going to embarrass you. Or try to steal him. Although I've always had a thing for Latin men." She smiled suggestively, flirting lightly, harmlessly. "You are Latin, aren't you, Alex?"

"Half," he answered, returning her smile. "My mother was Cuban."

"I thought so. I just want to know—"

"Carolyn?"

They all turned at the deep male voice.

"James." Carolyn released Alex's arm and moved to the other man's side. "There you are. We were just going to start looking for you."

He slipped a proprietary arm around her shoulders.

Kristen kissed him quickly on the cheek. "Happy birthday, Father."

"Thank you, Kristen. I'm glad you could make it." Then his gaze settled on Alex. "I don't think we've been introduced."

"Father, this is Alejandro Jamison."

Alex extended his hand, meeting and holding the other man's gaze as he made his quick, fatherly appraisal. "Mr. Helton."

James shook his hand briefly. "Kristen told us you run a shelter for boys in Miami."

"It's not actually a shelter, although sometimes it becomes that. It's really—"

James pulled a card from inside his tuxedo jacket. "Contact my accountant on Monday, he'll write you a check." To his wife, he said, "Come, dear, we need to attend to our guests. Kristen, I'm glad you could make it. Try stopping in to see your family a little more often."

Carolyn gave them an apologetic smile but let her husband lead her away.

Alex froze, anger washing over him in cold waves. He'd been dismissed.

"Alex?" He looked at Kristen and saw the concern in her eyes. "I'm sorry. He had no right—"

"Of course he did." Alex couldn't keep the resentment from his voice. "This is his house. You're his daughter. And I'm—"

"Don't." She pressed her fingers to his lips. "Whatever you were about to say, don't."

"Let's get out of here." He claimed her hand and started toward the French doors on the far side of the room.

Kristen let him guide her through the crowd, knowing if she stayed much longer, she'd have to go find her father. It had been years since she'd been this upset with him, but now wasn't the time for a confrontation.

Once outside, she took the lead, skirting the groups of people milling about the pool, and heading toward the path leading away from the house. As they worked their way along the narrow track, the sounds of the party gradually faded, and the whisper of water lapping against the sand eased her anger.

She'd known her father wouldn't take well to her seeing a man like Alex. That's why she'd told her parents she was bringing a friend and colleague—nothing more—from Miami. Her father, evidently, had seen through her ruse. And why not? He'd been down this road himself.

Finally, they came to the gazebo at the edge of the beach.

Releasing Alex's hand, she moved to the side facing the water. The night was sweet, with the heavy scent of salt and sea, and a nearly full moon trailing slivers of silver across the glassy surface of the Atlantic. She let the peace of this place wash over her, rinsing away her anger at her father.

"I love it here," she said.

Alex moved beside her and leaned against the railing. "I've never spent much time on beaches."

"Really?" She looked at him, surprised. "Even growing up in Miami?"

"It wasn't the thing to do." He looked embarrassed and turned back to face the ocean. "Not in my neighborhood."

The gap between their two worlds yawned ever wider, but Kristen turned away from it.

"When I was growing up," she said, "the beach was my retreat. Especially at night. I'd walk along the shore just out of reach of the waves. And I'd imagine the ocean was talking to me." She laughed lightly. "Silly."

"He's trying to protect you, Kristen." Obviously, Alex had let go of his anger too.

"Yes." She hesitated a moment before shifting to look at him. "Did I ever tell you about my mother?"

"You don't talk about your family much."

"Well, it's nothing very dramatic," she said. "But it might explain what happened in there."

He touched her cheek with the back of his fingers, sending sweet shivers through her. "Kristen, you don't have to justify anything to me."

"I want to."

He slid his hand to her hair, his fingers toying with the loose strands about her ear. "Tell me, then."

Closing her eyes, she gave herself up for a moment to his touch, to the feel of his hand in her hair. And forgot what she'd meant to tell him.

"Kristen?"

She opened her eyes and saw the hunger in his dark eyes. A hunger that mirrored her own. She took a step back, distancing herself. "My mother was a nurse."

"A nurse?"

129

She took a deep breath, steadying herself, and laughed lightly. "Can you imagine? James Helton, who traces his family lineage back to the *Mayflower,* and his money further, married Carolyn Darby of Jacksonville. A nurse."

"Bet that created quite a stir."

Kristen nodded and turned back to the ocean. "His parents nearly disowned him. But he stood up to them and married her anyway."

"That took guts." She could hear the admiration in his voice.

"Yes. And my mother paid the price." She glanced at him. "Oh, she had the man she loved, and eventually me. But they never let her forget she didn't belong."

"They?"

She made a sweeping gesture with one hand. "My father's relatives, his peers, the elite of Palm Beach."

"What are you trying to tell me, Kristen?"

She turned back to face him. "I guess I was just trying to explain why he's so protective of me."

"Or why things can't work out between us?"

The truth of his words struck her, but she shook her head. "No." She reached up as before and pressed her fingers against his lips. "Not tonight."

He captured her hand, turning it so he could kiss the inside of her wrist. "I understand what your father did, Kristen. Your mother is a beautiful woman. Almost as beautiful as her daughter."

She cupped her palm against his cheek, bringing her other hand up to rest against his shoulder. "Make love to me, Alex."

"We've been over this."

She slipped her arms around his neck and rose on her

toes to brush her lips against his. "I'm not asking you to marry me. Just make love with me."

He seemed to fight his own need—for a heartbeat, maybe two—then his resolve broke. He pulled her close, his mouth taking hers in a kiss that stole her breath.

A moment later, she pulled away, just enough to whisper against his mouth. "Take me back to Miami."

He studied her face for a moment. "Are you sure?"

She closed her eyes and rested her head against his broad chest. "Tonight, we live the fantasy."

Chapter Ten

Alex kept his distance and his silence on the long ride back to Miami. Surprisingly, Kristen hadn't questioned him when he'd taken the seat across from her in the roomy interior of the limousine. She, too, seemed lost in thought. Though he wondered if she really grasped the situation.

He'd just barely restrained himself on the beach. If they started again, he wasn't sure whether he could stop. One more caress, one more kiss, and he'd take her there, in the backseat of the limo, and to hell with propriety.

He tried to rein in his thoughts. Kristen deserved better than sex in the backseat. Hell, she deserved better than him. He needed to give her time to think, time to come to her senses. Something neither of them seemed capable of when they touched.

It was nearly one a.m. when they pulled up under the portico of her building. They waited in silence as the driver got out and circled around to open the door. Alex stepped out and offered Kristen his hand.

"Shall I wait, Mr. Jamison?" asked the driver.

Alex glanced at Kristen to see if she'd changed her mind. He found his answer in the bright green of her eyes.

"No," he answered, giving in to the desire rattling around inside him. "You can call it a night." He took Kristen's arm and escorted her into the building.

In the lobby, he released her arm, following her into the elevator when it arrived. He didn't dare touch her again. Not yet. Finally, the elevator stopped, and they stepped out into the cool white foyer, the doors shutting behind them with a soft whoosh.

Kristen fumbled with her purse and dropped her keys.

Retrieving them, Alex managed to open the door—though his own hands weren't too steady.

As they stepped inside, he asked, "Are we alone?"

"Yes." Her voice sounded strange, nervous, and she started toward the living room. "Would you like a drink? I've got—"

"Kristen?"

She stopped without turning, and he walked up behind her. Gently, he turned her around and lifted her chin so he could look into her eyes. "We don't have to do this. It's okay to change your mind."

"It's too late. We sent the driver away."

He laughed softly and stroked her cheek. "I don't need a driver. I can find my own way home."

"No." She closed her eyes briefly and brought her hand up to press his against her face. "Don't go. I want you to stay."

"Are you sure?"

She smiled slowly. "Yes. I'm sure."

"Okay." He folded his fingers around hers. "Then, no, I don't want a drink or something." He dipped his head for one brief taste of her. "I just want you."

133

He should have known it wouldn't be enough, that brief brush of lips. He wanted, no, *needed* more. And she came willingly, eagerly, her mouth seeking his as he pulled her into his arms. It was like every other kiss they'd shared—hot, eager, devastating—yet like no other. There was an added sense of expectancy, an understanding that this time they were going to make love.

After a moment, he pulled away, just enough to whisper, "Not here."

She nodded, her earlier nervousness gone, and took his hand. She led him up the stairs and down a hallway to her bedroom. She went in first, crossed to a bedside table, and switched on a lamp, sending soft light throughout the room.

When she turned back to face him, anticipation drifted between them like the first wisps of smoke before a fire. Slowly, she lifted her hands to her hair, pulling pins and letting them fall, until a riot of bright curls floated about her shoulders.

Alex ached to close the distance between them, wind his fingers into that soft cloud, and bury his face against its sweet scent. But he remained motionless, unable to move.

She reached behind her, and the sound of a zipper echoed through the silent room. For a moment, she held the dress with one arm braced across her breasts, while lowering the tiny straps from her shoulders. Then she paused and smiled seductively before letting the dress slip to a puddle of green silk at her feet.

Alex groaned.

Underneath, she wore some dangerously sexy, feminine concoction of creamy silk and lace, with stockings that clung to her thighs as if by magic.

He stood there, just looking at her, letting his gaze drift over her body, from the pale swell of her breasts to the slim curve of her waist, past the triangle of silk hiding her sex and down the long length of her legs. He'd imagined her a million times, a million ways, since they'd first met. None of it compared to the reality.

She stepped forward, out of the circle of green silk.

Still, he didn't move.

Instead, he started on his own clothes, his eyes never leaving hers. He removed his jacket and tossed it aside, unfastened his tie and the cummerbund at his waist, and unbuttoned his trousers.

Kristen's stomach tightened as Alex pulled out his shirt-tail. For weeks, she'd longed to explore his bare chest, to run her hands along the broad expanse of skin and muscle. Now he teased her by leaving the shirt on, but open, where she could catch only glimpses of what lay beneath.

"Come here," he said, his voice no more than a whisper.

She crossed the room hesitantly, stopping just within his reach. But he didn't touch her as she hoped. Instead, he took his time and knelt on one knee and took hold of her calf. With tantalizing slowness, he skimmed his hand down to her ankle, lifted it, and removed her shoe. He lingered, caressing the sensitive skin of her arch before shifting to the other leg and repeating the process.

Without releasing her, he looked up at her and smiled. A sexy, devastating smile that tightened around her heart. There was a boyishness to him she'd never seen before, a delight that seemed fresh and eager.

Then he slid his hands upward, sending shivers of desire racing up her thighs, and stopped at the tops of her stockings.

Kristen nearly groaned.

As he dipped his fingers beneath the hidden elastic, he laughed quietly. "Magic." Taking his time, he peeled off one thigh-high stocking, then the other. By the time he'd finished, the need within her had spiraled to new heights.

Finally, he stood, and she reached out to touch him, to stroke the warm male chest that teased her from beneath his shirt.

He caught her wrist. "I'm not done."

It was sweet torture, not knowing what he'd do next. Where he'd place his hands. What he'd take off. Something of hers? Or something of his?

"Alex?" It was almost a moan, almost a plea.

Grinning, he traced the line of silk covering her breasts. "What do you call this?"

She almost couldn't answer, almost couldn't get the words past the tightness in her throat. "A merry widow."

Again, he chuckled softly. "More like a widow maker. It could stop a man dead in his tracks." He skimmed his hands down her sides to where the merry widow stopped and her panties began. "How does it come off?"

She started to reach behind her to the hook and eye closures, but he stopped her.

"No," he said. "I want to do it."

He turned her around, and she heard his sharp intake of breath. Wrapping an arm around her waist, he pulled her against him, pressing his arousal against her backside while stroking her bare buttock.

"If I'd known you were wearing this"—he slipped a finger under the thong—"we'd never have made it off the beach."

Kristen let her head fall back against his shoulder, a sense of feminine power settling within her, right next to the heat, the damp ache accumulating between her thighs. "It's so I don't have any lines under my dress."

"Like hell," he growled. His mouth came down on her

neck while he pressed against her stomach, anchoring her tighter against the hardness of his groin. "You wore it to drive me crazy."

She trembled as he nipped at her neck, a deep feminine need building within her. He moved his hand down to cup her through her panties, and she moaned.

"Alex . . ."

"What is it, *chica?*" He caressed her with his voice even as he worked magic against the silk between her thighs. "What is it that you want?" He slid his hand inside her panties, and she arched against him.

"I always knew you'd be hot, Kristen. It was in your eyes." He delved farther, dipping inside her and pulling a groan from her lips. "But who knew . . ." He kissed her neck again, sending fresh shivers down her spine in rhythm with the movement of his fingers.

"Don't fight it," he whispered.

She couldn't—not even if she'd tried. The tremors started deep within her, building to a crescendo that would carry her over the edge.

"That's it, Kristen." He held her close, murmuring against her ear as she lost the last measure of her control, her climax shattering about her.

For several moments, he just held her, soothing her with whispered words while she drifted, lost between pleasure and embarrassment. She'd never responded so strongly to a man's touch, never felt herself totally lose control. She'd known sex would be different with Alex, better, more potent, but nothing had prepared her for what he could do with a few kisses and his deft fingers.

"Are you okay?" he asked softly.

She nodded, embarrassment heating her cheeks. He was still fully clothed, while she'd just lost herself.

He made quick work of the hooks down her back and dropped the merry widow to the floor. Then he turned her and lifted her. Closing her eyes, she wrapped her arms around his neck and rested her head against his broad shoulders as he carried her to the bed.

He left her then, or so it seemed. For suddenly she was cold where she'd been hot. Opening her eyes, she watched him rid himself of clothes.

The sight of his powerful chest roused her desire again, but it paled next to her response when he stepped out of his slacks. He was her fantasy: broad shoulders, narrow hips, muscular arms and legs. But she wanted more than the body. She wanted the man.

"Alex?" She held out her hand.

He took it and lay his long body next to hers. "Don't worry, *chica*." He nipped at her mouth as he quickly eliminated her thong, her last remaining article of clothing. "We're going to start all over again."

Kristen moaned and closed her eyes.

Alex had never wanted a woman as much as he wanted Kristen. She was so incredibly beautiful and more responsive than he'd ever dreamed possible. But his desire for her was only a shadow compared to another, stronger need. He wanted to make her remember. After she'd gone back to her safe white world, he wanted her to remember *him.* To remember this night.

He started at her throat, gently caressing her long, slender neck, the darkness of his skin a sharp contrast to hers. He cupped her breast, teasing the nipple with the pad of his thumb. It responded instantly, puckering against his palm.

"You're so beautiful," he whispered, and lowered his

head to touch the swollen peak with his tongue. Briefly. A mere flick, and it tightened further.

She wove her fingers into his hair, holding him near, silently begging him for more.

He obliged her, closing his mouth around the whole nipple, sucking and licking, and then turned his attention to the other breast. But it wasn't enough. He wanted all of her. He wanted to sheathe himself inside her and feel her come apart around him.

He wanted her to remember.

"Alex . . ." she said.

Lifting his head to look at her, he read the desire in her eyes. He lowered his mouth to hers, claiming her lips. Then he shifted, parting her legs and moving between them. He broke the kiss then, and caught her face between his hands.

It was time.

"Look at me," he said.

She nodded, her green eyes cloudy with desire and something else. Something warm and tender that pulled at his heart.

"Love me, Alex," she whispered.

He buried himself within her, very much afraid she wouldn't be the only one who'd never forget this night. "I do."

* * *

Alex eased his arm from beneath Kristen's head, careful not to wake her. He rose from the bed and made his way to the windows. Not that he could see much. The darkness of sea and sky was nearly complete, though he suspected it wouldn't be long before the first hint of gray touched the eastern horizon.

He'd started the night with the best of intentions. Or so he'd told himself. He'd wanted one night with Kristen, one evening when they could imagine things were different. Pretend *he* was a different kind of man. He hadn't intended on carrying the fantasy so far, on making love with her.

Or had he?

For weeks, they'd been fighting the chemistry between them, just barely avoiding acting on their desires. He guessed he'd always known that as long as they were around each other, it had been inevitable. Eventually, the fire between them would ignite.

He glanced back at the bed.

He'd had his fair share of women. Since he'd been old enough to know what sex was all about, there had been girls on the street, as ready and eager as he'd been for a little warmth and comfort. Later, there had been the women attracted to the soldier, and even a few he'd cared about for a while. But he'd never known a woman like Kristen, someone who set his body on fire even as she wove a spell around his heart.

Someone totally beyond his reach.

In the dim light, the differences between them seemed less pronounced. He could almost convince himself that they didn't matter. The contrasting shades of their skin and the places of their birth meant nothing. Her family and friends wouldn't care that she belonged in Palm Beach, while he made his home on some of the worst streets of Miami. She'd never suddenly realize, and regret, the kind of man she'd become involved with. In the cool darkness of this room, he could almost convince himself.

Almost.

Soon enough, the sun would rise, and reality would return with the searing Florida sun. He and Kristen didn't belong together—no matter how much either of them might wish that weren't true.

It was time for the fantasy to end.

* * *

Kristen woke to bright sunshine and an empty bed.

It didn't surprise her, though she wished it did. He'd left, and she could only guess at the reasons why.

Fear, maybe?

Though she'd never thought of Alex as a coward, what they'd shared the previous night had been intense. Possibly too intense for a man used to being on his own. However, she didn't really think Alex's desertion was due to fear of commitment or caring. She'd seen how he'd given freely of both to the boys at his youth center.

No, his fear went much deeper. It had to do with her background, with the mansion in Palm Beach and all it stood for. She and Alex had grown up in two separate worlds: hers, rich and powerful; his, poor and desperate. With a few brief words, her father had made that painfully clear to Alex. So had she, innocently and in her own way with her parents' story.

No, Alex wasn't afraid of caring or commitment. He feared Kristen and the world she'd come from. He'd left her before she could leave him. Because in his mind, that was the only way their relationship could end.

She wasn't going to let him get away with it.

She loved him, and somehow she'd prove it to him. Meanwhile, if nothing else, the chemistry between them was on her side. He wanted her as much as she wanted him. She'd seen that last night. And if that was all she had, the only way she could keep him near her, then she'd use it.

An hour later, she found him on the basketball court behind the youth center, playing a hard and fast game with several teenage boys. As before, she stood back and watched, admiring the slick sheen of his muscled chest and legs, the quickness of his movements. Only this time, she knew the feel, the taste of him, and it made it so much harder just to watch.

The game broke up and the boys scattered, leaving Alex to approach her alone. Kristen rubbed her damp palms against her shorts, the first twinges of uncertainty creeping up on her.

"What are you doing here?" he asked.

"Funny thing about that." She tried to sound nonchalant, unaffected by his dark scowl. "I woke up this morning. Alone."

"Aren't you usually?"

She met his gaze for a moment, but then had to look away. The coldness in his eyes hurt too much after what they'd shared. "You should have stayed."

"What's the matter, *chica?* Didn't you get enough?"

His crudeness stung, heating her cheeks, even though she knew what he was trying to do. She wouldn't let him drive her away like this. Defiantly, she forced herself to meet his hard gaze. "Did you?"

He laughed abruptly, scornfully. "You think it was that good? That I'd want a white-bread woman like you more than once? Yeah, I had enough." He turned and started to walk away.

"Liar."

He stopped and spun back around to face her. "What did you say?"

"I called you a liar."

He closed the distance between them in two quick

strides, and it took all her willpower not to back up. "You should watch your mouth."

"I'm not afraid of you, Alex."

He backed her against the wall. "You should be."

"You don't fool me anymore. I know you. I know your strength and your kindness." She rested her hand on his bare chest and could feel his rapid heartbeat beneath the warmth of skin and muscle. "I know your heart."

Cursing, he knocked her hand away and backed up. "That's where you're wrong, Kristen. You don't know the first thing about me. And if you did, you wouldn't come around here asking for more."

Hard words, but his eyes betrayed him. She saw his anger and his agony, the effort this act cost him. And underneath, she saw his desire.

She lifted her hand back to his chest and felt his sharp intake of breath. She looked into his eyes, ignoring the warning in their dark depths. "As for your question. No, I didn't get enough. Not nearly enough."

"So you enjoy slumming it? Making it with a ghetto rat?" The words were still wrong, but the vehemence had left his voice. "For how long, Kristen? How long?"

Her other hand seemed to move of its own accord to join the first, and for a moment she let her eyes follow the path of her fingers across his sweat-slick skin.

"I don't know." She shifted closer, bringing her breasts near enough to brush against his chest. "Does it really matter?" She worked her hands up to his shoulders and toyed with the damp hair near his collar. "I care only about now."

With a low growl, he grabbed her waist and pulled her against him. "Do you know what you're saying?"

Winding her arms around his neck, she rose up on her

toes and brushed her lips against his. "For however long it lasts, for however long you still want me."

Alex couldn't fight it anymore. He brought his mouth down on hers, claiming her. He wanted her too much, and she knew it. For the moment, nothing else mattered: not the fact she wouldn't stay, nor that she'd rip his heart out when she left. He wanted her and would love her until she sent him away—when the novelty wore off. Or she discovered the real man behind the facade.

Chapter Eleven

Kristen didn't understand why she let her cousin Gregory talk her into things. It had always been that way between them. Since she was a little girl, she'd gone along with him and usually ended up regretting it. Still, he was her cousin and the closest thing to a brother she had. So, when he practically begged her to accompany him on an evening cruise out of Ft. Lauderdale, she couldn't refuse.

"It's the latest thing," he'd insisted. Not that the "latest thing" had ever interested Kristen much, but he used the argument anyway. "The yacht is small but absolutely scrumptious. The food is adequate. But the entertainment . . . You're going to have to see it to believe it."

"I don't know, Gregory, I—"

"You *must* go with me, Kristen. It's been so long since we've spent any time together. You've been so busy with your career." He made "career" sound like a dirty word, and she figured that was probably the way he thought of it.

"It's only one evening," he insisted. "A Saturday night.

Certainly you can spare a few hours for your favorite cousin."

"My only cousin."

"As I said."

She groaned.

He'd used the one argument he knew would sway her. Guilt. Despite their eccentricities, she loved her family and often felt like she neglected them. They hadn't taken well to her busy schedule during the long years of medical school, and now the clinic absorbed most of her time.

"Okay," she relented. "I'll go." Besides, Alex had already told her he would be tied up that night. Some youth center business he needed to take care of.

"Good, I'll send a limo for you."

"That won't be necessary, I'll drive."

"Of course it's necessary." She could picture him rolling his eyes at her foolishness. "I refuse to let you arrive in that vehicle of yours. Besides, the yacht won't wait for us. It sails on time, whether you're there or not. And if I know you, you're likely to get involved at the clinic or—"

"Okay, Gregory," she interrupted, laughing despite herself. "Send the limo."

"Good. Now, remember, it's black tie."

"Don't worry. I'll do my best not to embarrass you."

But by Saturday afternoon, she regretted making the commitment. The day had been crazy, the clinic busier than usual, and by the time she got home, she wanted a long bath, a glass of wine, and an uninterrupted evening. She barely had time for a quick shower. That done, she pulled on a shimmery blue slip-dress and let her hair hang free. Her curls would be wild and uncontrollable, and Gregory would hate it. She smiled at the thought.

Somehow, she managed to make it downstairs to the lobby by the time the limo pulled up in front. Fortunately, the ride was restful, and by the time they arrived in Ft. Lauderdale, she was beginning to look forward to the evening. She enjoyed spending time on the water, and it had been too long since she'd gone out with any of her family. Besides, if nothing else, an evening with Gregory was always interesting.

The limo turned into a private marina off the Seventeenth Street Causeway and pulled into the parking lot. When the chauffeur opened the door, Gregory was waiting for her.

He smiled as he took her hand. "Perfect. You look absolutely perfect."

The compliment surprised her. She'd expected him to complain about her hair. He preferred a slick, sophisticated look on the women he escorted—even his cousin. "It's okay, Gregory. I'm here." She let her suspicions echo in her voice. "You don't need to continue flattering me."

"But you look great, and the evening has just begun." He had a strange glint in his eye that set off warning bells in her head. She knew her cousin. Once he'd gotten what he wanted—which was having her come on the cruise—he should have backed off. Instead, he seemed as excited and animated as he'd been while trying to convince her to join him.

"What are you up to, Gregory?"

"Me?" He looked properly offended.

She wasn't fooled. "This isn't some trick to introduce me to the perfect husband or something, is it? Because if it is, I'm really tired of everyone playing matchmaker."

"Believe me, Kristen, I'm definitely not trying to marry you off. Especially tonight."

He took her arm and led her up the gangplank of a yacht named the *Dusty Rose*.

It was every bit as lovely as Gregory had told her. Nearly a hundred feet long and with three decks, it combined modern convenience and comfort with the old-world charm of teak and polished brass. Young male waiters, all tanned, muscular, and dressed in crisp white shorts and T-shirts, circulated through the fifty or so well-dressed guests with trays of champagne and hors d'oeuvres.

A half hour later, they got under way.

The *Dusty Rose* headed out the inlet at Port Everglades into the Atlantic and then due east, away from the coast. Kristen stood with Gregory on the open top deck watching the Ft. Lauderdale skyline sink into the western horizon as the last rays of pink drained from the sky behind it.

"We're going out into international waters," Kristen commented.

Gregory shrugged. "There's gambling downstairs before dinner. Not much. A couple of tables."

"Is that the fabulous entertainment you promised me?"

He put an arm around her and gave her shoulder a squeeze. "That's just an appetizer."

After a while, they went down to the main deck, where dinner was served. Kristen had been on quite a few yachts in her life, privately owned or leased for an evening like this one. None could have claimed more elegant service or finer food. No wonder this particular evening cruise had become so popular.

As usual, her cousin had surrounded himself with a variety of wealthy socialites whom he took immense pleasure in baiting. And he was in rare form tonight. He'd start a controversial conversation and defend one side vehemently.

Until someone agreed with him. Then her versatile cousin would switch opinions quicker than you could blink.

Although she was enjoying herself more than she'd expected, by the time dinner ended, Kristen was again feeling the effects of her long day. Leaning over to Gregory, she said, "I'm going to one of the cabins and lie down until we dock."

"But it's time for the entertainment."

"I think I'll pass." She stood, and he rose from his chair as well.

Slipping his arm through hers, he said, "You can't desert me now, Kristen. This is the highlight of the evening. The *coup de grâce*. The *pièce de*—"

"I get the picture, Gregory."

"Come on, then. Everyone's heading up on deck. We have to hurry if we want to get a good spot."

"On deck?"

"You have something against open-air entertainment?" He squeezed her arm. "You can rest later. In the limo, all the way back to Miami." He smiled beseechingly. "I promise you won't be sorry. You've never seen anything quite like this."

"Why don't you tell me a little something about it?"

"That would ruin the surprise."

She couldn't imagine anything getting her jaded cousin this excited. She finally gave in out of curiosity.

"Okay, I'll come up for a while," she said, wondering why she always let him talk her into things she really didn't want to do.

Along with the rest of the guests, they made their way to the upper deck, where rows of wooden folding chairs had been arranged around a roped-off area. It seemed a strange setup to entertain a group of wealthy socialites dressed in cocktail dresses and tuxedos who'd paid two hundred dollars a person for the evening.

"Gregory," she said as he led her to a front-row seat and sat next to her. "What is this?"

"Patience, Kristen." He patted her hand. "You'll see."

Just then, the lights dimmed, and a spotlight focused on a man with a microphone as he stepped into the center of the roped-off area.

"Friends," he bellowed. "Are we ready to meet tonight's gladiators?"

The crowd cheered, and a sick knot formed in Kristen's stomach. Gladiators? This was a fight. She started to stand, but Gregory's hand clamped down on her arm.

"Stay," he ordered in a tone of voice she'd never heard him use before. "You have to see this."

Her anger flared; he'd duped her. "You know I hate fighting."

"Oh, I know, Kristen, I know. That's why you're going to want to see this one."

"No, I—"

"In this corner," called the announcer, "is our challenger." The spotlights switched to a man climbing over the ropes. "He comes to us all the way from LA. The West Coast's undefeated champion after thirty matches. Carl the Cruel."

The crowd cheered.

"And in the far corner," the announcer continued, "is South Florida's reigning champion. An ex-Army Ranger who has remained undefeated in twenty rounds. Ladies and gentlemen, I give you Alejandro."

It was as if someone had kicked her in the stomach.

Sinking back onto the wooden chair, Kristen watched

the man walking to the center of the ring. Alex. Her Alex. Wearing a pair of skintight black biker shorts and a tank top.

"Okay, folks," called the announcer. "Place your bets."

The crowd frantically began waving money at several men, who circulated with fists full of dollar bills, taking bets.

"He fills out those pants pretty well," Gregory whispered. "Wouldn't you say?"

Kristen whirled toward him. He'd planned this. He'd brought her here on purpose to show her Alex in this place. "Why did you bring me here?"

"I just thought you might want to know who you were sleeping with," he said.

She could have slapped him, would have if the announcer hadn't started again, drawing her back around to face the ring.

"Okay, folks," he said. "Time's up. All bets are placed. Let's begin."

It was like nothing she'd ever seen, though she'd heard about this type of thing. Two men, highly trained, performing for them like roosters at a cockfight. Gladiators.

Why would Alex do this?

Though she knew the answer without asking. Money. Alex needed money for his youth center. That didn't excuse it, she told herself. Nor the lies he'd told her.

The two men circled each other, and Kristen watched for a moment, fascinated. Warriors. Fighting for the amusement and entertainment of a bunch of bored, wealthy people with nothing better to do with their time and money. Until the first blow fell, then she couldn't watch anymore.

Yanking her arm from Gregory's grasp, she stood and pushed her way through the crowd, heading for the stairs.

Before she could reach them, however, the crowd let out a tremendous roar, drawing her back around to face the ring.

Alex stood over his opponent, arms raised in triumph.

Spinning back around, Kristen hurried down the stairs, away from the madness.

* * *

As the announcer pulled his arm up in triumph, Alex saw a riot of red curls and a flash of blue near the stairwell. He recognized her immediately, though for a moment he didn't want to believe it.

Kristen. She was there. She'd seen the fight.

Forgetting everything else, he broke free and headed after her. Sal made a grab at his arm.

"Alex, where are you—"

He brushed past the small man without a word.

The crowd went wild, parting for him as he ran toward the stairs. Someone else reached them first, a man, and it took Alex a moment to recognize him. Gregory. Kristen's cousin. And Alex immediately knew what had happened. Her family wanted to make sure she knew the kind of man she'd become involved with.

"Damn!"

On the main deck, he encountered one of the hired thugs the people who ran this circus kept around. He made the mistake of grabbing Alex's arm.

"Hey, Jamison," he said. "Where the hell do you think you're going?"

Alex wrenched free, backing the man up against the bulkhead. The man raised both hands palms-up as if in surrender. "Easy, boy. I ain't looking for trouble."

"Where did she go? The redhead in the blue dress."

"Didn't see no redhead . . ."

Alex grabbed the man by the collar and slammed him up against the wall. "Don't mess with me."

"Hey, man, take it easy. She said she wanted a private cabin where she could lie down. Said she was tired." He chuckled. "Of course, when that other fellow came after her, I got the idea—"

"Which way?" Alex pressed a little harder.

"The lower deck."

Alex released the man and headed for the stairs. When he reached the bottom deck, he knew immediately which cabin she'd claimed. Gregory stood guard duty at the door.

"She doesn't want to see you," Gregory said the moment he saw Alex.

"Too bad." Alex tried the door. It was locked. He knocked hard twice. "Kristen, I want to talk to you."

Nothing.

He rattled the door. "Kristen. Open this door."

"I told you she wouldn't talk to you," Gregory said.

Alex rounded on the other man. "This was your doing. You brought her here."

"She deserved to know."

Alex flinched at the hard truth. "Then why not just tell her? Why"—he made a sweeping gesture with his hand—"bring her here?"

"She might not have believed me otherwise. Besides, letting her see for herself was much more effective. She won't have anything to do with you now."

Alex clenched his fist. He'd like nothing more than to bury it in this man's face, but that wouldn't get him anywhere—especially not any closer to talking to Kristen. Spinning on his heel, he headed back to the locker room to change into some decent clothes.

The boat would be docking in about an hour. She'd have to come out of her cabin then, and he'd be waiting. He'd make her listen to him. Then if she told him to take a hike, he'd go without protest. First, though, she'd hear him out.

But he'd underestimated her determination to avoid him.

An hour later, when she came out of the cabin, he couldn't get anywhere near her. With Gregory at her elbow and surrounded by several armed thugs and a dozen more guests, he couldn't get within twenty feet of her.

He stood on the deck and watched as she made her way down the ramp to the waiting limo. Just before getting in, she looked back at the yacht, her gaze colliding with his for one brief, painful moment.

Then she was gone. Whisked away into the hot tropical night.

* * *

At first, the night watchman in Kristen's condominium wasn't going to let Alex wait. It was strictly forbidden for unexpected visitors to linger in the lobby. But over the last few weeks, the man had gotten used to Alex coming and going at all hours, and it turned out the old guy was a bit of a romantic. After Alex explained that he and Kristen had quarreled, the guard decided it wouldn't hurt if Alex hung out in the breakroom behind the front desk. There was coffee, a television, and a short couch where he could stretch out. The man promised to wake him the moment Kristen got in.

Alex tried to sleep but gave up shortly before dawn.

He wandered into the men's room and splashed cold

water on his face. Then he caught sight of himself in the mirror: the hollow eyes, ragged with lack of sleep, and the cut on his right cheekbone that attested to the previous night's disaster.

He tossed the towel in the basket and cursed his own stupidity. He would give anything if he could turn back the clock and change things. Only he wasn't sure what exactly he'd change so things would turn out different, so he wouldn't be waiting for the only woman he'd ever loved, knowing he didn't have a chance in hell of regaining her trust.

He stepped back into the lobby and heard voices: a soft feminine voice, strained and weary, and the old man, anxious and apologetic.

"I hope it was okay, miss," he was saying. "I thought you'd want me to let him wait."

Alex picked up his pace, rounded the corner, and came face-to-face with Kristen.

Chapter Twelve

Alex came to a dead stop, caught by the sight of her. Despite the lines of fatigue etched in her face and the pain haunting her eyes, she looked incredible. Cool, elegant, and beautiful. And further out of his reach than ever.

"Oh, here he is," the guard said. "Mr. Jamison, I was just telling Dr. Helton—"

"It's okay, Joe." She raised a hand without looking at him, without once taking her eyes off Alex. "I was expecting Mr. Jamison." To Alex, she said, "I suppose we need to talk. Shall we go upstairs?"

He nodded, lost for words now that he'd finally gotten close enough to speak with her.

As they stepped into the elevator, she said, "I stayed at my parents' last night."

He'd guessed as much. Her family would have gathered around her like hens around a chick, protecting her from danger and consoling her for making the mistake of consorting with a man like him. A common street fighter.

The image left a bitter taste in his mouth.

"Does that hurt?" she asked.

At first he didn't know what she meant, and then he realized she was referring to the gash on his cheekbone. "No," he answered.

"I don't suppose you've had anyone look at it."

"It's not that bad."

"I have antibiotics upstairs. They'll keep it from getting infected."

He didn't care about the damn cut, but the coldness in her voice stung. Especially since he'd put it there.

When they reached the stark white penthouse foyer, the door to the apartment opened and the maid stepped back as they entered. "Good morning, Dr. Helton. Mr. Jamison."

"Good morning, Maria," Kristen said. "Could you bring us some coffee? We'll be out on the terrace."

"Yes, ma'am."

"Kristen," Alex started. "Wait."

"Not yet, Alex." She held up a hand to cut him off, much as she'd done to the man downstairs. "I need to change." She motioned toward the French doors in the living room. "Go on outside. I'll get something for your face and be out in a minute. Then we'll talk."

She'd dismissed him as easily and quickly as her father had done the night of his party. It should have infuriated him. Instead, a piece of him died inside. He had no one to blame but himself.

Kristen left Alex standing in the foyer.

She couldn't help herself. She needed a few more minutes alone to gather her strength and her resolve. When she'd first seen him downstairs in the lobby, she'd almost lost both. She'd almost thrown herself in his arms and begged him to hold her.

Almost . . .

She couldn't let herself be sidetracked by her feelings. Or by his. She knew what she had to do. She'd spent a sleepless night coming to the painful decision, and the long ride back from Palm Beach hardening her determination. She just wasn't ready to carry through with it.

Upstairs in her bathroom, she pulled off the clothes she'd borrowed from her mother and slipped into a pair of well-worn shorts and a T-shirt. Funny how over the last month she'd gained a fondness for comfortable, old clothes. So much had changed since she'd come to live in Miami. She'd changed. Or had she? Maybe it had all been an illusion. Something she'd made up to please Alex. She wasn't sure of anything anymore. Especially her motives where he was concerned.

Grabbing her medical bag, she checked to make sure she had everything she needed. Then she couldn't put off facing him any longer. Taking a deep breath, she headed back down the stairs.

She found him stretched out on a lounge chair, his eyes closed and a cup of coffee balanced in one hand. She felt a tug at her heart just looking at him. Despite everything, she still loved him. Unfortunately, she'd learned last night that love wasn't enough.

"Alex?" She said his name softly, not wanting to startle him. She knew he hadn't gotten any more sleep than she had last night. Joe, the night doorman, had told her Alex had spent the night on the old couch in the breakroom.

He opened his eyes, his dark gaze focusing on her.

She turned away. Setting her bag on the table, she opened it and pulled out the items she needed. "I hope you're not going to give me a hard time about taking care of that cut."

"No."

"Good. Otherwise it could get infected, and—" She abruptly stopped her flow of words, realizing that she'd begun to ramble, talking about unimportant things while shying away from what she really wanted to know.

"How long has it been going on?" she asked, still not looking at him. "The fights?"

He hesitated briefly before answering. "About eight months."

Eight months. He'd been lying from the beginning, pretending to be something—someone—he wasn't. She opened the bottle of peroxide and dampened a cotton ball. "Is LJ in on it?"

"No. No one else."

She took a deep breath and turned to move up beside him, hoping he wouldn't notice the way her hands trembled.

He grabbed her wrist, stopping her before she could touch him. "I had no choice, Kristen. They were going to shut down the center."

She pulled her hand free and dabbed at his swollen cheek. "There are always choices."

"What do you know about it?" Anger edged his voice. "Look at you. Look at this place."

She stopped her ministrations and stepped back. "Is that what this is about? My money?"

"No, dammit!" He pushed himself out of the chair. "It has nothing to do with you or your money. It's about the center and wanting to keep it open so bad I'd have done anything."

For a moment, he glared at her, reminding her of the

man she'd seen last night. The stranger who'd stepped into that ring, ready to literally fight for his dream. Then his anger drained away, replaced by a look of desperation.

"Have you ever wanted something you couldn't have, Kristen? Something you wanted so badly, it became not only your dream, but your every waking thought?"

She met his gaze straight on. "Yes." *You.*

Neither of them spoke, the tension circling around them like the gulls overhead. She almost lost her resolve again, seeing his pain. His hunger. He still wanted her, she could see it in the dark depths of his eyes, and felt the echo of that need in herself. But she'd already made the mistake of thinking they could ignore the wide gulf that separated their worlds.

Finally, she broke the spell by turning to put away the peroxide and retrieving the topical antibiotic. "Sit down," she said.

For a moment, she thought he'd refuse, and then he sat in one of the straight-back chairs. She applied the ointment to his face and covered the cut with a butterfly bandage. When she was done, she moved around to the other side of the table, putting distance between them.

"It's a shallow cut," she said. "It should heal cleanly."

"Thank you." He sighed and briefly closed his eyes. "Kristen—"

"I know why you did it, Alex. I even understand that you thought you had no choice. What I don't understand is why you lied."

His dark gaze bored into hers. "I never lied to you."

She laughed abruptly, bitterly. "I guess that's true. Technically. You never said you weren't spending your free time participating in gladiator fights."

"And what if I'd told you? Would you have said, that's

great. Go ahead. Earn money for your boys any way you can."

"No, I—"

"You would have what, Kristen? Written me a check?" He stood abruptly. "Dammit, don't you see, I don't want your money. I just wanted to keep the center open."

Silence descended between them again. Harder this time. And colder.

"Besides," he said, a dangerous edge to his voice, "the problem isn't that I didn't tell you about the fighting. It's that I don't fit in your neat vision of the world."

He was right, and she hated herself for it—though she couldn't admit it to him without losing control.

"So that's it," he said when she turned away, unable to speak. "It's over."

She shook her head but couldn't look at him. "I don't know."

"Now who's lying?"

"I . . ." She opened her mouth to object but couldn't find the words.

He grabbed her chin and forced her to look at him. "It seems I was right all along, Dr. Helton. You can't handle the truth or deal with the real world. As for you and me . . ." He released her and took a step back. "We never really existed."

* * *

Kristen managed to hold back her tears until he'd gone, until the front door of the apartment closed, and she heard the soft whine of the elevator starting its descent. Then she couldn't fight them any longer. They came softly at first, a steady stream of individual teardrops staining her cheeks.

It wasn't until she'd closed herself in her room that she

gave way to the great racking sobs that shook her body. She kept telling herself she had done the right thing. She'd listened to everything her family had said last night, and then she'd thought it all out carefully. She'd made her own decision.

The gulf between her world and Alex's was too wide. If they continued trying to bridge it, they'd spend their lives hurting each other. Like she'd hurt him by taking him to her parents' party, and he'd hurt her last night when she'd seen the man she loved walk into that ring.

She had to let him go. She knew that.

Then why did it feel like she'd never stop crying? Why did it *feel* wrong?

* * *

Alex spent most of the morning driving.

At first, he didn't even think about where or how far. He put the van in gear and headed up the coast, along A1A amid the Sunday morning beach traffic. He left Miami and Ft. Lauderdale behind and continued north, past Lighthouse Point and Hillsboro. Then he came up on a stretch of beach with parking alongside the road and pulled over, sitting for several minutes, staring out the window at the bright blue Atlantic.

He thought of the night in Palm Beach with Kristen, how she talked about walking along the beach whenever she needed to get away and think. Pulling off his shirt and shoes, he climbed out of the van and made his way across the hot sand to the water's edge. He stood for a moment, letting the gentle rush of the tide lap around his ankles. Then he started walking, again heading north, without allowing himself to think. He only felt. The wet sand beneath his feet. The brutal sun against his bare back. The ache in his heart where he'd kept his love for Kristen.

Suddenly he knew what he had to do.

He couldn't let it end like this, couldn't let Kristen go without a fight. Despite everything, despite the vast differences between them, they had something special.

They loved each other.

How often did anyone find love? Once, maybe twice in a lifetime if you were lucky. And once found, who could afford to throw it away? If he and Kristen let all the rational reasons why they shouldn't love each other stand in their way, they'd regret it for the rest of their lives.

He couldn't get back to the van fast enough. He broke into a run, hoping he wouldn't hit too much traffic going back south. This time, he'd take Kristen into his arms and kiss her until neither one of them could think. Until all they could do was feel.

Then they'd see if either one of them could walk away.

Chapter Thirteen

I t was early afternoon before Kristen pulled herself out of her tears. She needed sleep, but that wasn't an option at the moment. Too much had happened. Her mind wouldn't allow her to rest. So she sought solace in the one thing that had never failed her. Work. The clinic was closed on Sunday, but there was always paperwork or reading to do.

A half hour later, she'd made it across town and parked in front of the deserted building.

The minute she stepped through the front door, however, she sensed something was wrong. She waited and listened, but heard nothing. Deciding she must be imagining things, she started across the waiting room, and then stopped. She heard it again; a small sound, no more than the shifting of a tree against the building. Except it came from inside.

Fear pricked the back of her neck.

Quietly, she backed up, remembering everything she'd ever heard about getting out of a building if you thought there was even a remote possibility of an intruder.

The door slammed behind her.

Spinning around, she nearly collided with a teenage boy who looked vaguely familiar.

He grabbed her arm. "Where ya going, *Doctora?*"

"What are you doing in here?" She managed to pull away, adrenaline giving her strength. "The clinic is closed on Sunday."

As if from nowhere, a silver blade appeared in his hand and snapped open. "That so?"

Her heart picked up its pace, and she glanced toward the door.

"You'll never get there." He grinned, as if daring her to try.

"What do you want?"

"Come on." He waved the knife toward the rooms behind her. "Back there."

When she didn't move right away, he grabbed her arm again and spun her around, shoving her forward. All the way down the hall, her mind raced. There had to be a way out of this. Some protection against this boy and his knife.

"In there," he snapped when she reached the supply room.

She stopped, and he pushed her inside.

Hector stepped out from behind a supply cabinet where he'd evidently been hiding. She realized then where she'd seen the boy with the knife. He'd been with Hector the day her car had been stolen.

Hector's eyes darted from her to the other boy. "Raoul, what the hell are you doing, man?"

Raoul shoved her farther into the room, and she caught herself against a countertop. "She was gonna call the cops."

Hector closed in on him, dark eyes flashing dangerously.

165

"You weren't supposed to let her see you. Then we wouldn't have to worry about her calling no cops."

"Well, she saw me, all right?"

"No, it's not all right."

"Look, Hector, this is crazy," Kristen said. "Stop this before it goes too far. Leave now and there's no harm done. I won't say anything—"

"Shut up." Raoul waved his knife at her, but Hector knocked it aside.

"Put that thing away," he commanded.

Before Raoul could respond, two other boys hurried into the room, obviously drawn by the sound of angry voices. "What's going on?"

"We need to get out of here," Hector said, nodding toward Kristen.

"We ain't got what we came for." Raoul stepped between Hector and the other two boys. "The man said—"

"Shut up," Hector said, cutting him off.

He glanced quickly at Kristen, and she realized he hadn't wanted her to pick up on that particular piece of information. But it was too late. She'd heard, and it made her think of her conversation with Detective Langford. He'd suspected someone of stealing from the clinic, and he'd been right. Now she knew there was someone else, a man working with these kids, someone behind whatever they'd come here to steal.

Alex?

She dismissed the idea as quickly as it surfaced. Alex might risk his own physical well-being to keep the center open, but he'd never resort to stealing or selling drugs. It would defeat everything he'd worked for, everything he stood for.

"Raoul's right," said one of the other boys. "We need to get the stuff."

"Forget it," Hector interrupted. "It's too late."

"What about her?" Raoul said. "We can't just leave her here."

"We'll tie her up."

"What good will that do? She can identify all four of us."

"They won't find her until morning," Hector said. "By that time, we'll be long gone."

"No way, man." Raoul took a threatening step toward Kristen. "I ain't running just cause some nosy *gringa* got in the way. I say we take care of her right now. Dump her body in the Glades. No one will ever find her."

"Are you crazy, man?" Hector grabbed Raoul's arm. "You want to commit murder?"

"You ain't got the guts, Hector? I'll do her." He moved in closer, but Hector stepped in front of him.

"I ain't killing no one."

"You don't have to. I'll do it."

* * *

Alex tried Kristen's condominium first.

She wasn't home, and neither the doorman nor her maid would give him any information about where she'd gone. He knew she wouldn't go back to Palm Beach—no matter how upset she'd been. She might be willing to walk away from him, but he'd come to understand over the past weeks that she'd never desert the clinic and the people who'd come to depend on her. He left a message and decided to try the clinic. One way or the other, he would see her today.

As he turned onto the street next to the clinic, he saw

her car parked out front. He smiled in relief. This was even better than he'd hoped. They could talk without worrying about anyone else listening in.

He parked the van behind her car and climbed out.

To his surprise, the front door opened when he tried it, bringing him to a standstill. All his senses went on alert. If Kristen was in here alone, she would have locked the door. Quietly, he stepped into the waiting room and pushed the door closed without clicking it shut. Then he started slowly down the hall.

When he heard voices, he came to a dead stop.

"What's wrong with you, man?" Alex knew that voice. Raoul. One of Hector's more unsavory friends. "You gone soft?"

"I'm not going to let you do this," Hector said. "Give me the knife."

A chill slipped down Alex's spine.

He inched forward, enough to peer around the edge of the door into the room. The sight tightened the icy fear around his heart. Three of the four boys faced Hector, who stood between them and Kristen.

Raoul had a knife.

"Get out of my way," Raoul demanded. "Or I'll cut you too."

Hector held his ground. "You can try."

Alex edged forward, his attention on Raoul and the knife.

Then Kristen saw him, a slight gasp escaping her lips, and for a fraction of a second, Hector's attention shifted to Alex.

Raoul chose that moment to lunge.

Hector moved quickly, stepping between Raoul and Kristen, taking the knife in his side.

168

As Kristen clutched at Hector, sliding to the floor with him, Alex threw himself at Raoul, knocking the knife from his hands. Before Alex could grab the boy, however, he fled with the two others.

Alex started after them.

"Let them go," Kristen called. "I need you here."

He hesitated briefly in the doorway but came back, kneeling down beside her as she tore off Hector's shirt. Bright red blood bubbled from his left side with a soft hiss. Alex caught Kristen's quick, worried glance, but she didn't have to tell him the prognosis. Raoul had punctured Hector's lung.

"What can I do?" Alex asked.

"Call 911 and get an ambulance here. Then get me a stack of gauze pads and a pressure bandage from the cabinet in the corner. They should be on the middle shelf."

When he returned with her supplies, she held the remains of Hector's shirt tight against his side.

"Hang in there, Hector," she said.

"It hurts like a bitch."

"It feels worse than it is." She took the gauze from Alex, replacing the bloody shirt with several pads. "You're going to be all right. I promise."

He nodded, biting on his lower lip as she applied pressure.

"Alex," she said, never taking her eyes off the boy. "Get me some blankets and a pillow from the other room."

By the time he got back, she had the pressure bandage in place around Hector's rib cage to keep the lung from collapsing. Together, they covered him with a blanket and put a pillow beneath his feet in case he went into shock.

"I'm so sorry, Hector," she said, her voice breaking for the first time. "This is my fault."

Alex started to object, but Hector beat him to it. "No sweat, *Doctora*. Raoul and I . . ." He tried to smile. "We were gonna come to blows soon enough anyway."

"But if I hadn't—" she started to say, but Alex reached across and took her hand.

"Hector's right, Kristen." He squeezed her hand, trying to reassure her with a touch, with the love he felt for her. "You can't blame yourself. Besides"—he looked at Hector—"he's going to be fine."

The boy grimaced in pain, just as a high-pitched siren announced the ambulance's arrival. Nothing had ever sounded so good.

The next few minutes were crazy as the paramedics rushed in. Alex kept back, out of the way. They lifted Hector onto the gurney, but Kristen never let go of his hand.

"I'm going with you," she assured him.

They were still securing him when Frank Langford showed up, flashing his badge and working his way to Alex's side.

"What happened here?" Langford asked.

"Dr. Helton interrupted some kids breaking into the clinic. Hector happened along just in time." He caught Kristen's quick glance of surprise. "Took a knife in the ribs for her."

Langford looked doubtful. "Gonzales just *happened* along?"

"Lucky thing."

"Give us room," one of the paramedics said, and started to move the gurney toward the hall.

Alex stepped back, falling in behind as they wheeled Hector toward the front door.

Langford followed. "What about you, Jamison? What's your part in all this?"

"I was looking for Kristen and got here just as it was all going down." Alex didn't spare the man a glance; all his attention was on Kristen and Hector. "I was too late to do anything."

"Uh-huh." He looked at Kristen. "What do you have to say, Dr. Helton?"

She glanced at Alex briefly. "That's how it happened, Detective. Now, if you have further questions, you'll have to wait until later." The paramedics lifted the gurney into the ambulance, and she climbed in beside it. "I have a patient to take care of."

* * *

Kristen couldn't block her fear. Not while Hector remained in surgery. Though the doctor in her knew his injuries could have been much worse, no knife wound to the chest area was minor. The part of her that had watched a boy step in the way of her death couldn't be easily reassured.

LJ had brought Elena and Luisa to the hospital, and Kristen sat holding the older woman's hand while they waited. Nobody spoke. At one point, Kristen wondered who was comforting whom. It made her feel for the first time like she truly belonged there, with these people. With Elena and Hector, LJ and all the others who'd accepted her into their neighborhood and their lives. She'd made a difference. Hector had shown her that.

Mainly, however, she realized she belonged with Alex.

Though why that seemed so clear now, when less than four hours ago she'd let him walk out of her life, she couldn't say. Except she knew if given another chance, she'd never let him go. Any problems or differences they had could be worked out. Life was too precious to throw away such a special opportunity to love. However, no one seemed to know where Alex was, and that gave her more to worry about. Had he chased after the other boys? If so, he could be hurt or injured himself.

Finally, the doctor came out of surgery, announcing Hector would be fine. Kristen felt a sense of relief for the first time since that knife had plunged into his side. The four of them were allowed in to see him, but she and LJ hung back as Luisa and Elena took up their vigilance on either side of the unconscious boy.

It was a several hours later, after Hector had awakened, before Alex finally showed up, entering the room with dark, worried eyes. Kristen's sense of relief quickly faded as she met his gaze and knew something else had happened.

LJ must have sensed it too. Moving to Luisa's side, he said, "Let's get some coffee."

Luisa glanced at Alex, searching his face, but finally nodded and stood, walking to her mother and taking her arm as well. As they made their way toward the door, Alex stopped them with a hand on Luisa's shoulder. "I'll take care of him. I promise."

She smiled grimly and let LJ lead her out the door.

When they'd gone, Alex made his way to Hector's side. "How are you feeling?"

"How you think I feel, man? Like a stuck pig."

Alex smiled—though Kristen could see he'd forced it—and sat on the edge of the bed. "That's what happens when you play with knives."

Hector laughed abruptly.

"Look, Hector, what you did back there—"

"It was nothing, man."

Alex looked at Kristen, and she felt the warmth of it steal over her. "You're wrong. You saved Dr. Helton's life."

172

He shifted his attention back to the boy. "And I consider that a personal favor."

"Yeah, well . . ." Hector glanced briefly at Kristen as well. "I owed her."

Alex took a breath, and she saw his hesitation. Whatever he'd come to say, he would prefer not to. "They picked up Raoul and the other boys."

Hector didn't respond.

"They're saying you planned the whole operation," Alex continued.

Again, Hector kept quiet.

"So far," Alex said. "The doctors have held Langford at bay. But . . . pretty soon he's going to be in here asking questions."

Hector turned away. "I ain't got nothing to say to him."

"Unfortunately"—Alex glanced at Kristen, a plea for support in his eyes—"you don't have a choice. You can demand a lawyer, but sooner or later you're going to have to talk to the police."

Kristen took Hector's hand, trying to reassure him, but not knowing how. She could see what was coming and didn't know how to stop it. How to help this boy who'd saved her life.

"I heard what you told Langford," Hector said, finally looking at Alex. "About my just happening by."

"I owed you." Alex shrugged. "But Langford's not buying it. Not with the other boys saying different."

Hector let out a short, humorless laugh. "He wouldn't believe it anyway."

"Hector," Kristen said tentatively, suddenly remembering something. "At the clinic, Raoul mentioned a man. Was there someone else involved?"

"You wouldn't believe me if I told you."

Kristen squeezed his hand. "I'll believe you."

Again, he hesitated. "Langford. He was my contact. He told me how to get into the clinic, what to look for. And he was the one who was going to pay."

Kristen looked to Alex, who'd gone perfectly still. "You're sure about that?" he said.

"Of course I'm sure." Irritation crossed Hector's face.

Alex ignored it. "Would you be willing to testify to that?"

Hector glanced at Kristen before looking back at Alex. "I don't know."

"I'm no lawyer," Alex said. "But I think you've got a lot going for you. You're underage, and you saved Kristen's life. The district attorney might grant you immunity."

"We'll get you a lawyer," Kristen added. "I know some of the best in the state." When they both looked at her, she added, "It's the least I can do."

"It's a possible way out," Alex said. "And at this point, you might not have any other choice. It's either him or you." He paused a moment before adding, "I'll back you either way, Hector. It's up to you."

"I've got to think about it."

"Sure." Alex nodded. "Meanwhile, LJ and I will hang around outside just to make sure Langford doesn't try anything stupid."

"You really think they'll grant me immunity?"

"As I said, I'm no lawyer. But, yeah, I think they will."

Hector considered for a moment longer, and then said, "Okay, I'll do it."

Alex smiled, this time for real. "Okay. I'll go contact the district attorney's office."

"Wait a minute." Kristen pulled a scrap of paper from her purse and scribbled a name on it. "This is one of the best criminal attorneys in the state. Call and tell him I want him to take care of this."

Alex stood unmoving, not taking the offered paper. For a moment, she thought he'd refuse and would try to handle it himself. But she wasn't going to take no for an answer, even if she had to make the call herself. This was between her and Hector, and she wouldn't let Alex's pride get in the way.

Then he surprised her by taking the paper. "He'll take the call on a Sunday?"

"If you use my name, he will."

He grinned at Hector. "Nice to have influential friends." To Kristen he said, "Okay, I'll give it a shot."

He started to leave, but Hector stopped him. "Wait. There's one other thing."

Alex turned back toward the boy.

Hector pursed his lips, looking embarrassed. "Langford promised that none of us would get blamed for the robbery." He paused again before saying, "He was gonna pin the whole thing on you."

When Alex returned, Kristen rose from her chair and met him at the door. "He's sleeping," she said.

Alex nodded, and they stepped outside the room. He looked exhausted, and she barely restrained herself from reaching out to touch him.

"I got hold of the lawyer you suggested, and he talked to the district attorney," he said. "They've picked up Langford. Seems they've been watching him for some time. With Hector's testimony, they can put him away."

"And what about Hector?"

"Since he saved your life and is willing to testify, the DA has agreed to grant him immunity."

Kristen took a deep breath and leaned against the wall. They'd done it. Or, more exactly, Hector had done it with a little help.

"You look tired," Alex said.

She smiled slightly. "And you aren't?"

"Come on, there's a patio off the waiting room. Let's get some air."

She glanced back at the room.

"Hector will be fine."

Nodding, she let Alex lead her away.

The outside air felt great, warm and heavy with the smell of the South Florida summer. They walked to the edge and leaned against the chest-high stone wall. For several moments, they remained silent. Things might have been settled for Hector, but between them, nothing had been resolved.

Finally, Kristen asked the one question that had bothered her all afternoon. "Alex, what were you doing at the clinic?"

"I came for you."

She turned to him, trying to read his expression in the dim light. "But I thought—"

He didn't let her finish. "Don't think," he said. "That's been our problem. We've been thinking too much."

Before she could say another word, he pulled her into his arms and kissed her, long and deep, with a tenderness that said more than a million words ever could. He kissed her until she couldn't think anymore. She could only feel.

When he finally released her mouth, he said, "That's what I came back to tell you, Kristen. I love you, and everything else is negotiable."

She looked at him, not quite believing that it could be that simple.

"If it's the fighting you're worried about," he said. "That's over. I should have found another—"

She pressed her fingers to his lips. He was right, they'd both been thinking about this too much, analyzing all the reasons why they shouldn't care about each other while ignoring the obvious.

"I love you too, Alex. As you said, everything else is negotiable."

Epilogue

Kristen stood at the back of the small, exquisite church in the heart of Little Havana and watched the street.

When she'd told her mother about marrying Alex and the small wedding they'd planned, Carolyn Helton had cried. Then she'd said she would talk to Kristen's father and try to convince him to attend. That had been three weeks ago. Kristen hadn't heard from any of her family since.

Alex came up behind her and touched her shoulder. "I'm sorry."

She looked up into his eyes and tried to smile. "I thought maybe . . ."

"I know." He brushed his fingers against the back of her cheek. "Give them time. They'll come around."

She nodded, wanting to believe it.

LJ walked up beside them. "We need to get started. Everyone's waiting."

Kristen forced a smile. "Looks like you've got two jobs today," she said to LJ as she slipped her arm through his. "Alex's best man and father of the bride."

"Are you sure you're okay?" Alex asked.

This time, she smiled for real. No matter what happened with her family, she couldn't regret her decision to marry this man. She loved him too much. "I'm fine. Go on."

He hesitated a moment longer, then nodded and started down the side aisle to take his place at the front of the church. A squeal of brakes stopped him, and they all three turned toward the church's front doors.

A black stretch limousine pulled up at the curb, and Kristen's heart leapt. LJ steadied her as the driver got out and circled around, but before he could reach the door, it sprang open and Gregory stepped out, followed by her parents.

Gregory reached her first.

"Well, cousin," he said. "Better late than never."

Kristen laughed through her tears and hugged him. "I'm just so glad you came."

"Wouldn't miss it for the world." She thought she heard a bit of emotion in his voice but decided she must be hallucinating.

When she released him, he turned to Alex and held out his hand. "Well, Alejandro, you're not who I would have selected for her, but then, you can't pick your relatives, can you?"

Alex hesitated a moment, and Kristen shook her head, knowing her future husband and Gregory would probably never understand each other. Then Alex surprised her. "No," he said. "You can't. But we'll get used to each other."

Gregory laughed.

"Kristen?"

She turned toward her mother, who'd entered the

church on her father's arm. Beaming, Carolyn stepped away from her husband and hugged Kristen fiercely.

"I threatened to divorce him," she said not too softly. "It gave him the excuse he needed to give in and come."

Kristen grinned, knowing the chance that either of her parents would even entertain the thought of a divorce was almost nil. "Thank you, Mother."

Carolyn went to Alex next and kissed him on the cheek. "Good luck. You're going to need it." Then she took Gregory's arm. "Shall we be seated?"

They started down the aisle, and her father moved up beside LJ. "I believe this is my job."

LJ released her arm and quickly backed away. "Yes, sir."

Then her father zeroed in on Alex. "I have just one bit of advice for you, young man. Kristen is my daughter. If you ever hurt her, you'll answer to me."

Alex responded without missing a beat. "In a few minutes, she's going to be my wife. So I suggest you remember your own advice, or I'll be coming to see you."

Kristen rolled her eyes and slipped her arm through her father's, realizing Alex was going to fit into her family just fine.

"If you two are done posturing," she said, "do you think we could get on with the wedding? I'd really like to get married sometime today."

Alex grinned and gave her a quick kiss. "The sooner the better."

Note from Pat

I hope you enjoyed Rough Around the EdgesLoving and will try another book in the series. Also, please take a moment and leave a brief review of the book to help spread the word. Thank you.

Just follow the link. Rough Around the Edges

About the Author

Patricia Keelyn writes contemporary romance and romantic suspense.

She's published twelve novels and several short stories independently and for the three major publishes, including: Ballantine, Bantam, and Harlequin. Her last three books were hardcover suspense novels released under the pseudonym Patricia Lewin.

Pat also teaches writing workshops and classes in various formats and length around the country at at her coral Community College.

For more information or updates:
Pat's Website
Pat's Reader List

Join and follow Pat on: Facebook, Goodreads, and Bookbub.

facebook.com/PatriciaKeelyn

Patricia Keelyn Books

THE PROTECTORS
Collection
PATRICIA KEELYN

Loving Lindsey

Rough Around the Edges

Running for Cover

Nobody's Hero

Becca and the Beast

A Mother's Heart
Collection
PATRICIA KEELYN

Keeping Katie

Once A Wife

Where The Heart Is

Box Set

Patricia Lewin Books

Blind Run Collection

Blind Run

Blind Run Short Stories

Hide

Away

Erin Baker Series

Out of Reach

Out of Time

Standalone Short Stories

Helen Told Me

www.ingramcontent.com/pod-product-compliance
Lightning Source LLC
Chambersburg PA
CBHW020633180626
46816CB00003B/951